THE BEAT

Missing Person

The burglar's gloved hands were inches away from Mum's sleeping face. He was unarmed. Clare took a deep breath and lifted her truncheon.

"Don't move," she told him, as her parents' eyes blinked open. Dad, in his pyjamas, sat up as Clare continued talking.

"I'm a police officer and you are under arrest. You do not have to say…"

"Clare," Dad shouted suddenly. "Look out!"

Clare turned. But it was too late. A heavy object struck her on the head and she fell to the ground.

Other titles in the Point Crime series:

Kiss of Death
School for Death
Peter Beere

Avenging Angel
Final Cut
Shoot the Teacher
David Belbin

Baa Baa Dead Sheep
Jill Bennett

A Dramatic Death
Margaret Bingley

Driven to Death
Anne Cassidy

Overkill
Alane Ferguson

Death Penalty
Dennis Hamley

Concrete Evidence
The Smoking Gun
Malcolm Rose

Look out for:

Break Point
David Belbin

The Beat: Black and Blue
David Belbin

POINT CRIME

THE BEAT

Missing Person

David Belbin

Scholastic Children's Books
7–9 Pratt Street, London NW1 0AE, UK
a division of Scholastic Publications Ltd
London ~ New York ~ Toronto ~ Sydney ~ Auckland

First published by Scholastic Publications Ltd, 1995

Text copyright © David Belbin, 1995
Cover illustration © Mark Taylor, 1995

ISBN 0 590 55904 4

Typeset by TW Typesetting, Midsomer Norton, Avon

Printed by Cox & Wyman Ltd, Reading, Berks.

10 9 8 7 6 5 4 3 2 1

For Mum and Dad

The city in these pages is real. The events described in them are not. All of the characters, together with the police station where some of them work, are imaginary. The author wishes to thank the many people, including serving police officers, who helped him with this series. He alone is responsible for any mistakes.

1

Clare kept waking up. Distant church bells told her the time: one, two, three … she ought to be able to sleep. Her shift didn't begin until two the next afternoon. She could have a lie-in.

The night was quiet. When Clare got up to go to the toilet, it felt cold, as though this might be the first frost of the year. She got back into bed and pulled the warm duvet tightly around her, willing sleep to come.

Her mind began to fuzz over. As Clare slipped out of consciousness, she became a different girl, the one she had been the summer before last: a university student, with nothing more important to worry about than her overdraft. She was about to move out of a hall of residence into a flat with friends. Her younger brother, Angelo, was teasing her about which sex her friends were.

Suddenly, she woke. There was a noise, and it wasn't church bells. She was nearly sure that it was coming from downstairs. Clare had the attic room. Noise from the street outside rarely disturbed her. Someone was walking about on the floor below, moving things.

There was probably an explanation. It would be Mum, rummaging in the bathroom cabinet for a pill, or Dad, who was prone to insomnia, getting out some papers that he needed for work. But Clare wasn't sure. She got out of bed, putting on her dressing-gown this time, as well as her slippers. Then she had another thought and went to the dressing-table, where her uniform was laid out. She fumbled around until she found what she was after – a wooden baton, smaller than a baseball bat, but just as effective.

Quietly, she walked downstairs.

As she reached the landing, Clare saw that her parents' door was slightly ajar. That was unusual. One of them must be up. But the scraping noise she could hear didn't sound like Mum or Dad. Then she saw that there was a light on in her younger brother's bedroom. Mum and Dad never went into Angelo's bedroom. Not since…

It was definitely a burglary, Clare decided. She had two choices. She could go downstairs, call the police, and risk being heard by the burglar. He (it was always a *he*) might then escape, attacking her if she tried to get in his way. *Or* she could try to arrest him.

Caution is the better part of valour. Clare decided to wake Mum and Dad. There was a phone in their room. She and Dad could tackle him while Mum dialled three nines. Clare pushed the bedroom door fully open, taking in the sweet odour of sleeping people. She reached in and switched the light on.

"Dad!" she hissed. "You've got to wake up! We're being…"

Then she saw him. Thin, white, with a balaclava on his head, leaning over Mum's dressing-table, lifting the wooden box which she kept her jewellery in. The burglar's gloved hands were inches away from Mum's sleeping face. He was unarmed. Clare took a deep breath and lifted her truncheon.

"Don't move," she told him, as her parents' eyes blinked open. Dad, in his pyjamas, sat up as Clare continued talking.

"I'm a police officer and you are under arrest. You do not have to say…"

"Clare," Dad shouted suddenly. "Look out!"

Clare turned. But it was too late. A heavy object struck her on the head and she fell to the ground. The burglar with the jewellery box trod on her chest as he ran out of the room. Clare was dimly aware of

Dad stumbling over her, going after them. She wasn't sure how much time passed. Then Mum was helping her to her feet.

"Are you all right, love? Are you badly hurt?"

"Only my pride," she told Mum, sitting up. She felt her head. It was bleeding.

"I was stupid," Clare went on. "I'd heard the other one, in Angelo's room. But it was a shock, seeing that bloke standing there. I reacted without thinking."

Dad came up the stairs.

"They had a car," he said. "Doors open, engine running…"

"Did you get the number?" Clare asked. Dad shook his head.

"Ford Escort. Dark blue."

"Probably stolen," Clare muttered.

Mum was dialling the police, talking, repeating Dad's description of the Ford Escort. At this time of night, Clare knew, the roads were very quiet. There was a fair chance that a patrol car would pick the thieves up. Either they would be caught in the next ten minutes, or, most likely, they would get away with it.

"They'll be here soon," Mum said.

Then she stooped to pick up the empty jewellery box from the carpet. There hadn't been much in it, Clare knew that, but there was a bracelet and brooch which had been Mum's grandmother's.

Both were gone. Clare put her aching head into her hands, knowing that she wouldn't get any sleep now. It was going to be a long day.

The city was dead. A boring Sunday night, dragging itself into Monday morning. When it was this quiet, the hours really dragged. There were still three of them to go. Then home for a quick kip and on again at two. It was a dog's life.

"Burglary in Bobbers Mill. Suspects escaping in dark blue Ford Escort. Two young men: one white, one black."

"5117 responding."

Ben Shipman took the address and picked up speed. He was only a minute away, but didn't go to the house yet. Instead, he cruised the boulevards: Gregory Boulevard, Radford Boulevard, as far as Lenton Boulevard, where he turned back. Nothing. Not even a taxi.

Somewhere, not far from here, two toerags were unloading a blue Ford Escort. If they had any sense, they would garage the car, then dump it in the morning when there was plenty of traffic about.

Ben was twenty-three years old and two weeks into his probation period as a copper. Technically, he shouldn't be out in a Panda on his own. His Detective Training Officer wouldn't approve. But the shift was short-staffed tonight, and Ben had yet to be lined up with his new "mentor" – the bloke who would show him the ropes, starting tomorrow – correction, this afternoon.

He said his badge number into the radio.

"5117. No sign of offenders. I'm going to the house."

Probably, the people who'd been burgled would be annoyed that it had taken him fifteen minutes to respond to their 999 call. But the way Ben saw it, comforting the victims took second place to catching the villains. He was after results.

The road was a quiet one, cut off at both ends so that it took Ben an extra two minutes to find it. He got out of the car. In the street stood a paunchy, middle-aged man wearing a dressing-gown. In an Italian accent he introduced himself as Nick Coppola.

"Did you get a good look at them?" Ben asked.

"Not really, they both had balaclavas on. My daughter saw more than I did. They were lads, I think, late teens. The one whose face I saw – the one who hit my daughter – he was black."

"What kind of black?"

Witnesses often had trouble describing people of colour.

"Not an Asian, he was ... what do you call it?"

"Afro-Caribbean? Like me?"

The man nodded.

"Yes. Like you. Only..."

"Only what?"

"Only not quite as dark."

Ben wrote these answers down in his notebook.

"Have you had time to see what's missing?"

"Not a proper look. They've taken my wife's jewellery, my wallet, the video, obviously. They left the TV."

"Perhaps you could have another check while I interview your wife and daughter. Their names?"

"Maria and Clare. This is Clare."

A girl was standing at the bottom of the stairs. She was wearing a towelling dressing-gown. Thick black hair. Pretty. Good figure, too, from what Ben could see. She looked vaguely familiar.

"Clare Coppola?"

She half smiled, like she recognized him too.

"He hit you?"

"It's nothing."

She showed him the bruise, which was near her ear. There was a little blood. Soon, it would ripen to a deep red.

"Do you know what it was?"

"I think it was my brother's computer. The main bit, you know, the hard disk. Anyway, it's not there now."

Ben raised an eyebrow.

"Your father didn't mention a brother. Did he see either of these men?"

"Angelo's dead," Clare explained. "He was killed in a car accident last year."

"Ah." Ben fumbled for the appropriate words. "I'm sorry."

"It's all right," Clare told him. "You weren't to know."

She described the burglar she had seen and took Ben up to the bedroom, where her mother was trying to make a list of what had been in her jewellery box.

"He was standing there," Clare pointed. "I was standing here."

Ben looked down at the small patch of blood on the carpet. Then he saw what was right next to it.

"Did one of them drop that?" he asked.

"No," she told him. "It's mine."

Now he remembered where he had seen her before. At Ryton. In training. She must have been in the intake directly after his.

"That's right," she told him, with an embarrassed look on her face. "I'm a police officer."

2

Neil Foster got to the parade room at ten to two. He'd been on a late the night before and only got five hours sleep. He hated these changeovers. They played havoc with your stomach. His mother had forced a full can of farmer's broth down him when he got up, half an hour before. Now his stomach felt tight and heavy. He would be like this all day: nerves knotted and no appetite. It went with the job, so much so that Neil's mother nicknamed him "the Thin Man". Most people had trouble losing weight. Neil had problems putting it on.

Every shift started in the parade room, where the day's duties were allocated. In a shift of eight, a couple would be out walking, on the beat. Another couple would be in a car, double covered. Two or three would be doing paperwork. That left the sarge, who might be at the station or in a car with the spare body, depending what he had on that day. Now and then you saw the inspector, too, but he had four other sections to look after.

Neil didn't have any paperwork to do. He was hoping to be partnered in a car. The month before, he'd finished his two year probationary period. Since then, he'd done a two week course which qualified him to act as mentor to another new copper. Neil was hoping to be assigned the young black guy, Ben Shipman, whose previous tutor had been transferred. Maybe he'd hear today.

Ben and Neil nodded at each other across the table. They had had a couple of drinks together during Ben's last patrol at the station, and could become friends, Neil thought. Next to Neil sat John Farraday and Tim Cooper, both in their late thirties. They were explaining to the sergeant that they had to write up the ram-raiders from the week before. Then the boss walked in.

"Change of the guard, this week," Inspector Thompson announced. "My transfer to traffic finally came through. I'm off at the weekend." There was a round of applause. Thompson invited them all for a drink at the Old Rose on Saturday.

"Who're we getting, boss?" Tim Cooper asked.

"A new bloke. Not from this division. A promotion."

The inspector smiled.

"Anyway, I've got a parting gift for you. There're two probationers on this shift, so you'll be needing some extra experience…"

Two? Neil thought. Who was the other one? The boss continued.

"I'd like you to welcome back an old friend."

Neil looked up. Jan Hunt walked into the room, wearing her sergeant's stripes. She had been Neil's tutor officer, when he was in training. He hadn't seen her for three months, not since she came into the station to show off her first baby. Now, there was a round of greetings and banter. Neil punched her lightly in the stomach.

"You've put on weight."

She punched him back in the same place, hard.

"You haven't."

"How's Henry?" Inspector Thompson asked.

"He's fine. Only waking up once in the night now, thank God."

"Are you full time, Sarge?" Neil asked her.

She nodded.

"It was either that or a desk job."

Thompson left. Sergeant Cope smiled benevolently. It couldn't be comfortable for him, having another sergeant under his command. Especially one who, last year, ran his shift while he was off with back trouble.

"We're still a couple short," he said.

It was after two.

"Mike called in sick," John said. "Again."

The sergeant shrugged.

"Right then," he said. "Jan, take the car. I'm partnering you with young Ben here. Show him the ropes. See if you can do as good a job with him as you did with Neil last year."

"Yes, Sarge."

Ben and Neil shot each other glances.

"Neil, you're out walking – *when* our newest recruit shows up."

"Who?"

The sarge ignored the question.

"Inspector tells me that you asked to act as a mentor."

"That's right. I took the course. I was hoping…"

Their eyes met. Neil shut up.

"This was going to be Mike's job," the sarge said. "But he could be out for weeks. So, we're giving the new one to you … when she arrives."

"She?"

Neil heard a door opening, then a familiar voice.

"I'm very sorry I'm late, sir. There was…"

The sergeant looked up.

"No excuses. Just don't let it happen often. Clare Coppola, I'd like you to meet your mentor officer. This is…"

"We've already met," Neil said.

They exchanged a long, embarrassed look. Neil

had seen Clare in a uniform before. But then she had been working a different patch, during her first five week patrol, and he had been picking her up from work so that he could take her out in the long, summer evenings.

Then, she was his girlfriend.

Now, she wasn't.

She'd dumped him when she went back to Ryton for her second period of training. Last week they'd been meant to go on holiday together, to Centerparcs, in Sherwood Forest. He'd got the leave booked, and everything. Then she rang him up. *It's not that I don't like you,* she said. *I like you a lot. But it's getting too serious. I can't handle it.* Now she stood there. It was the first time he'd seen her in six weeks. She looked lovely, and very ill at ease.

"Hallo, Clare," Neil said.

Jan gave Clare a funny look. Jan wouldn't be happy to be in the same section as Clare. She'd been very unhappy at the way Clare interfered in the investigation of her brother's death last year. Neil had let Clare know too much about the case. It was the one real blot in his copybook during the two year probationary period. How could the sarge make him Clare's tutor? It was a bad joke.

Without speaking to Clare, Neil turned to Sergeant Cope.

"Is this the boss's idea of a leaving present?"

The sarge shook his head.

"The inspector knows nothing about it. It was his replacement's decision."

Just as Neil was about to say something else, the phone rang, and the sarge answered it. Ben Shipman, on his way out of the room, leant over Clare.

"Are you all right?" Neil heard him say.

Clare muttered something about casualty, then Ben left. He would spend the rest of the day in a comfortable car, while Neil and Clare would be getting cold. The sergeant put the phone down and spoke to Neil.

"Little job for you while you're out on your travels. Fifteen-year-old girl, Hannah Brown, not been seen since she went to bed last night. Call in when you're round that way."

"Can't the car do it?"

The sergeant shook his head.

"Not urgent. She'll probably have turned up by the time you get there. We all know about fifteen-year-old girls, eh?"

Neil nodded and smiled. Clare frowned.

"Better get a G.71," Neil told her.

"G.71?"

"A *Missing Person* form. Over there."

Clare went to the filing cabinet while Neil got them both a radio and did a signals check. She returned a moment later with the A3 form. She and Neil were alone in the parade room.

"What do we all know about fifteen-year-old girls?" Clare asked.

Neil smiled.

"Missing fifteen-year-old girls usually turn up with twenty-one-year-old lads," he told her. "Happens all the time."

Clare nodded, preoccupied. She followed him out into the street. It was a fine October day. Cold, but not too cold. The sky was blue, speckled with small clouds. The city air smelt fresh, sweet.

"Community policing," Neil said, slapping his hands together. "Don't you just love it?"

"It's OK," Clare mumbled, putting her hands in her pockets.

She had the extension mike on her radio strapped near her head. Big mistake, as far as Neil was concerned. Someone could strangle you with it. But presumably Clare knew that. She'd think he was being condescending if he pointed it out to her. They kept walking.

Neil said hello to a couple of people. A cyclist stopped them, and pointed out the large brick which someone had left right in the middle of the cycle track. Clare placated him, promising that they'd keep their eyes peeled for any other deliberate vandalism. Finally, when they got to a long stretch of empty road, Clare stopped and turned to Neil.

"What are we going to do?" she asked him.

Like it was *their* problem. Like there was a *them*.

"I don't know," he told her.

"You can't be happy about this."

"It's … awkward."

But already his mind was calculating how he could turn the situation to his advantage.

"You've got to say you don't want to be my mentor," Clare told him. Neil had been keeping his cool, but now he lost it.

"You've got a nerve. You're the trainee. If you don't want to work with me, fine. I never dreamt that you'd be transferred to this section. I was hoping to work with Ben. But you can go and see the boss, not me."

Clare shook her head and stared at the pavement. Then she mumbled.

"I can't do it again."

"Again?"

Clare explained.

"The tutor I had on my first patrol. Carl Price. I asked not to be put with him again."

"Why?" Neil asked, confused. "You told me he was all right."

"I didn't want you involved."

Clare looked embarrassed.

"Carl kept – you know – asking me out, making sexual innuendoes, the usual immature stuff."

"Why didn't you tell me?" Neil wanted to know. "You were my girlfriend. He knew that."

Clare got defensive.

"How would that have made me look? Running to my boyfriend at the first sign of trouble? You'd probably have tried to beat him up."

Neil felt anger surging up inside him.

"Maybe I still will."

"You're not my boyfriend any more," Clare told him, as if he needed reminding.

"And has Carl Price got something to do with that?"

Clare shrugged.

"All I know is that it made me realize I didn't want to mix my love life with my work life."

Neil couldn't believe what he was hearing.

"But you only joined the police because you were going out with me!"

"It wasn't as simple as that," Clare protested, sternly. "Look, Neil, I was confused – still am, I guess. I'm sorry we didn't work out. I'm twenty years old. You were my first serious boyfriend. I didn't know what I was doing. Still don't."

Neil stared at the ground, then half whispered, "I know what I want."

"Please, Neil, don't." Clare gripped the sleeve of his jacket. "Ask to be put with someone else. You can't like this any more than I do."

Neil broke free of her, saying nothing. At the moment, Clare was right. He didn't want to work with her. It seemed like a sick joke on him. But it was an opportunity, too. If they were forced to work together for five weeks, they would become closer. Maybe Clare would realize that she did still love him, after all.

Maybe.

3

It was a comfortable, modern, middle-class house. Hard to see why the Browns needed so much space when they only had one child: four or five bedrooms, built-in garage, burglar alarm. Clare wondered whether a burglar alarm would have stopped what happened at her house the night before. As they stood in the spacious porchway, Neil suggested that Clare should do all the talking.

"Useful experience," he told her.

At least he hadn't said what Carl Price would have said: *this job needs a woman's touch.* Meaning: *it's a waste of time.*

Mrs Brown was a well-groomed but tired-looking woman in her late thirties. She poured both officers a cup of tea.

"When did you last see your daughter?" Clare asked her.

"Last night. At ten, when I went to bed. She was still up."

"How do you know?"

"Her light was on. I could hear the TV in her room."

"And when did you notice she was missing?"

"This morning, when she didn't come down to breakfast. Ted, my husband – her stepfather – usually drives her to school. He went up to her room. The door was locked. There was no reply."

"This was at what time?"

"Eight."

"But you didn't phone the police until five past two in the afternoon," Clare said, in a neutral tone. "Why?"

"We knew that the police wouldn't do anything for twenty-four hours, so we looked for her ourselves … ringing round her friends, school…"

The twenty-four hour business wasn't strictly true, Clare explained. After twenty-four hours, the police had to put the missing person's details on to the national police computer. But sometimes the trail had gone cold by then.

"Naturally, we're very concerned at your daughter's disappearance. You say it's never happened before?"

"Never."

"And none of her friends can cast any light on the situation?"

"No. Nor can the school."

"Which school is that?"

"Greencoat. Everyone there says it's not like her."

"I'm sure. Mrs Brown, excuse me asking, but does your daughter have many boyfriends?"

Linda Brown didn't need to think.

"No. She sees boys, of course. She goes to a mixed school. But no one special. There was a boy, last year, but it wasn't serious."

"His name?"

Mrs Brown told them. She didn't know the address. Despite what the girl's mother said, Clare guessed that Neil was right – it would turn out that Hannah Brown had gone off with a lad. Still, there were some worrying aspects to the case. The most significant one was that Hannah hadn't gone missing before. OK, it didn't look like she'd been kidnapped, or assaulted – yet – but she was probably out of her depth, wherever she was. She was vulnerable.

Clare got out the G.71 form, and began to fill it in. This didn't take long. Hannah Brown had no marks, scars or peculiarities. There were, as far as Clare and Neil could tell, none of the "warning signals" which vanishing people tended to display. Hannah had no history of mental illness, no contagious diseases and had never been violent.

Nor, as far as her mother knew, was she suicidal, or involved in drug taking. Though, often, as they had taught Clare at Ryton, the parents were the last to know such things.

Hannah did not have a pronounced Nottingham accent – not many young people from this part of town did. Her mother described her personality as "usually cheerful. But she could be intense at times. She's very clever, academically." The recent photograph which Hannah's mother provided showed a girl with medium-length brown hair, wide eyes, and a fairly large, striking face. She would be easy to recognize, if you saw her in the street. Clare took a list of all the friends and acquaintances Mrs Brown could think of.

"Most girls in Hannah's situation do reappear quickly," she assured Mrs Brown, getting up to go. "We'll let you know if we hear anything at all, and we'd like you to do the same for us."

"Of course."

"Actually," Neil said. "There is one more thing."

"Yes?"

"I'm afraid that it's a rule, in cases like this. We have to search the house, make sure that your daughter isn't hiding somewhere on the premises. Is that all right with you?"

"Yes. Of course. Help yourselves."

"Is that really a rule?" Clare asked, when they were outside Mrs Brown's earshot. "Or have I been missing some signs? Do you think that she's killed her and hidden the body in the cellar?"

"It's a rule," Neil asserted. "And we may find something useful."

They went up to the girl's room. The door-frame was cracked where her stepfather had kicked the door in that morning. The room was nice, bigger than Clare's room at home. Hannah had her own TV and video in one corner. There was a pine dressing-table. Clare looked at the display of make-up and perfume spread across it: Dune, Coco, stuff that Clare couldn't afford to use herself, even though she was five years older than Hannah and in work. If Hannah left home for a boy, wouldn't she have taken her expensive perfume with her?

The window was open a crack. Clare opened it. She could see how Hannah would have been able to shin down the drainpipe beside it. On a nail sticking out of the wall was a small fragment of some kind of purple material. Clare reached down and got it.

There was an Aubrey Beardsley poster on the wall and a stack of CDs in a flashy, black, metallic tower. Neil examined them.

"These are filed alphabetically. There are gaps – she's taken a few out. Probably the ones which'd be easiest to sell. How much did the mother say she'd taken?"

"A holdall. A few clothes. Very vague."

Neil opened the wardrobe.

"Here's why Mum didn't know which clothes she took."

The white, fitted wardrobe was so full of garments that it would be impossible to keep them from getting creased. Neil pulled out a silk blouse with a designer label.

"What do you reckon?" he said, holding it out to her.

"I reckon that she's a typical, spoilt only child," Clare said – remembering, as she said it, that she was an only child herself these days.

"No. I meant the blouse. It'd look good on you."

Clare flinched, tossing back her hair.

"That's enough of that, Neil. We're working."

Neil was staring at her.

"What is it?" Clare asked.

"Where did you get that?"

"What?"

Neil reached out, pushing back Clare's hair to reveal the dark bruise behind her left ear.

"That."

"It's nothing."

Clare resumed examining the room. Schoolwork on the desk. Some magazines: *Just 17*, *Vox*, nothing unusual.

"Tell me about it," Neil said, coming closer, examining the bruise.

"It's embarrassing."

There was nothing to indicate that the girl even

smoked cigarettes, never mind took drugs. Not that that proved anything. If you believed statistics, half the fifteen-year-olds in the country were popping Ecstasy or LSD once a week.

"Tell me about it," Neil insisted. "Did someone do that to you, or was it an accident?"

Clare took a deep breath. He was bound to hear about it sooner or later. Better here than in the station.

"It wasn't an accident," she told him. "We were burgled last night."

The story didn't take long to tell.

"Dad and I spent half the morning looking at mug shots, so I've hardly had any sleep. Great start to my patrol, wasn't it?"

They continued to walk around the rest of the house. It was a formality. There was no need to concentrate.

"You mustn't let it get to you," Neil said.

"I'm trying not to," Clare told him. "Mine was the only room they didn't do, so it's not as bad for me. They took some of Mum's jewellery. And they turned over Angelo's room, took his computer and his radio. I think that's what's upset Mum and Dad the most. They'd left it, you know, exactly as it was."

"Maybe it's time to change that."

"Maybe it is, but that's a horrible way to ... it's just like they always tell you: when your house is burgled, it feels … desecrated, like it'll never be the same again."

"I'm sure the feeling fades," Neil said, kindly.

"Are you? How?"

Mrs Brown came out into the hallway before he could answer.

"Did you find anything?"

"Not really," Clare told her. "It seems fairly certain that Hannah left of her own accord. You haven't had any more ideas about where she could have gone, have you?"

"No."

"The holdall you mentioned earlier. What was it like?"

"A big, purple, cloth thing."

"How big?"

"She used to carry a tennis racket in it, and all her kit."

"We'd like to talk to your husband later," Neil said. "When does he get in from work?"

"It varies. He had a late start today because of looking for Hannah. Could I get him to call you?"

"Perhaps you could ask him to come into the station at about nine," Clare suggested. "We could take his statement then."

"I'll do that."

"Hannah's real father," Clare asked, almost as an afterthought. "She couldn't be…"

Mrs Brown shook her head.

"He died five years ago."

"I'm sorry. Were he and Hannah close?"

"Not particularly," Mrs Brown said, in a bitter tone. "He wasn't home all that much. I guess you'd call him a workaholic. And an alcoholic. He had half a bottle of scotch in him when he drove into the side of a lorry. I always blamed the job for getting him like that."

"I see," Clare said.

"No, you don't," the woman replied, bad-temperedly. "He was one of your lot."

"Our lot?"

"That's right. Hannah's father was a policeman."

Ben Shipman drove smoothly, too smoothly. He made every manoeuvre as though this was his advanced driving test. He was quiet, too – very different from Neil Foster, Jan's partner before she went on maternity leave. Neil asked questions all the time, especially at first. Ben said little, as though he were reluctant to reveal his ignorance on any subject. Getting him to relax might take a while.

They began to cruise back streets off the boulevards.

"Are we looking for something?" Jan asked.

"Dark blue Escort. Used in a robbery last night."

Jan remembered it from the bulletin board.

"Anything else on it?"

Ben shook his head.

"Witness got a good look at one of them, spent the morning checking out mugshots – no joy. One white, one Afro-Caribbean. Late teens/early twenties. That's all."

"Hold it."

Jan had spotted a car with no tax disc. They stopped. There was no sign of the owner. Jan did the paperwork. It took two minutes. They were by a phone box, so Jan took the opportunity to ring her child-minder, Dawn. It was the first time that Jan had been apart from Henry for more than an hour and she was worried about him. Dawn told her that Henry was fine.

Ben gave Jan a funny look when she got back into the car.

"Everything all right?" he asked.

"Yes. Fine. Look, this Escort. You reckon it was stolen?"

"Probably."

"OK. I know a couple of places where the thieves might've dumped it. Let's have a look."

They drove to a car park in the Meadows. No sane person would leave a car there. The small tarmacked area was surrounded by a maze of walkways which made escape easy and pursuit impossible. But there were no cars there, stolen or otherwise, so they drove on to a leisure centre car park. Joyriders took and left cars there all the time. They were easy pickings. A thief would see someone pull up and get out, carrying sports gear. They would know that they had at least an hour before the car owner returned.

"Over there."

Jan was confused. She couldn't see any dark blue cars. But then she saw what Ben had seen. Two lads: one was watching, but in the wrong direction. The other was leaning over a Volvo. Jan could guess what he had in his hands – two large screwdrivers. They were either stealing the car or nicking the radio. Jan got out. As she walked towards the boys, Ben parked the car so that it was blocking the car park exit. The boy with the screwdrivers opened the car door, reached in. As he was taking the stereo, the other one turned round and saw Jan. He grabbed his mate's arm and for a moment, both of them were looking at her. The look on their faces wasn't fear. It was irritation. They were fourteen, at the most. The robbery had taken them less than a minute.

"Hold it right there, lads."

They didn't stop to think about whether to give themselves up. Both of them ran, in different directions. Jan followed the one with the stereo in his hand. He was weaving his way through the cars towards the main road, trying to lose her. He was wasting his time. Jan knew where he was heading: towards the grassy mound which divided the car park from the exit road.

She called "Stop!" a couple of times, not very

loud, because she was having trouble getting her breath. It wasn't easy to run after someone when you were carrying all your police clobber. Harder when you were out of condition because you'd just had a baby. She was getting a stitch. Where was he? And where was Ben? The other one had been going in his direction. If Ben hadn't caught him, her partner should be in the car by now, ready to head them off.

She reached the road. Where was the kid with the stereo? Suddenly, there was a loud engine noise and a clattering behind her. A red Astra was coming over the grassy mound and back on to the pavement, right by her. Jan jumped out of its way. She saw the grinning boy, tracksuit hood pulled over his head, as he accelerated out of the car park. They'd probably left the car with the engine running. She'd been a fool not to think of that. Then she heard Ben shouting to her.

"Come on!"

He was in the Panda. Jan could see the other boy, sitting in the back seat, handcuffed. She got up and tried to run towards the car, but ended up staggering. The chase had taken it out of her. Ben gunned the engine, pushed the door open.

"Get a move on. We'll lose him."

Jan clambered in and they sped off. There was no sign of the red Astra.

"You should have gone without me," Jan muttered.

"Go without the sergeant? I couldn't do that," Ben said, driving off towards the ring road.

"Did you get the registration number?"

"I've radioed it in."

After five minutes, they headed back to the station. The weather had been good earlier, but now it began to turn grey. The boy in the back seat said nothing. Neither did Ben. They'd caught one of them. With a bit of work, they'd find the name of the other boy. Jan had got a good look at him. Even if the other kid didn't cooperate, they'd have enough to charge both of them. But Ben's attitude implied that getting one wasn't enough. He made Jan feel like this was her fault. If she'd been in better condition, he seemed to be saying, we'd have had both of them. She didn't need this kind of aggro. Something told her that this partnership wasn't going to be easy.

4

When Hannah woke up, she couldn't remember where she was. Something had happened. What was it? Then she recognized the room. She was at Amanda's. Hannah checked her watch. Gone four. Outside, it was getting dark. A whole day had gone by and she had nowhere to sleep tonight. There was a noise downstairs and Hannah trembled, remembering the night before. Then the door opened and Amanda walked in, still in school uniform. She switched on the light.

"God, Hannah, are you still here?"

"Sorry. I only just woke up."

Amanda sat on the bed beside her.

"No. It's all right. Only, my mum'll be home from work soon. If she finds you here…"

"Yeah. Sure."

Hannah tried to remember where she'd put her clothes.

"Was anything said at school today?" she asked.

"Miss Carter asked a few of us if we knew why you were away, if you'd been having problems, stuff like that. No one told her anything. Well they couldn't, could they? Look, we've got twenty minutes. I'll get you something to eat. Want a cup of tea?"

"Yeah," Hannah mumbled. "Why not?"

Hannah dressed in the clothes she'd left home in the night before. She could do with a shower but there wasn't time. She would have to get used to doing without. She joined Amanda in the kitchen.

"Where are you going to go tonight?" Amanda asked.

Hannah shrugged.

"I'll find somewhere. It's best if you don't know."

"Do you need any money? I've got a bit."

"I've got my cashcard."

"Is it safe to use that?"

"They can't watch every cashpoint machine in the city, can they?"

"I guess not. Well, if there's anything…"

Hannah interrupted.

"Can I come here in the day again, if I'm stuck?"

Amanda only hesitated for a moment.

"Course you can. But leave it a bit later. You only missed my mum by a minute this morning."

"I know," Hannah said. "I watched her leave."

"And what would you have done if she'd seen you?"

"I was calling for you on the way to school."

"Oh, sure, dressed like that."

Hannah was wearing Doc Martens, an old pair of jeans that were too tight and a loose, pea-green fisherman's sweater.

"I'd have said I had a field trip."

"Wouldn't have worked. Mum knows that we're in the same geography group. And she knows how long it takes to walk from your house. You'll need to think of better lies."

"OK."

Hannah finished her sandwich. Amanda looked at her watch. Hannah could tell that she was going to have another go at asking about what happened the night before. Then, just as Amanda was opening her mouth to speak, the doorbell rang.

"Can you get rid of them?" Hannah begged her.

"I'll try. Hide in the dining-room."

The dining-room was connected to the kitchen by a single door. Hannah picked up her bag and stood just inside the doorway. She could hear the conversation from the hallway.

"We're looking into the disappearance of Hannah Brown. I believe that she's a friend of yours."

"Yes."

"May we come in?"

"Er, I guess…"

Hannah swore silently. She remembered the kitchen table. There were two mugs and a plate on it. *Two* mugs. Breathing deeply, she opened the door, went in, picked up her mug, and hurried back into the dining-room, spilling some of the tea on the way. Don't let them notice the brown stain on the floor, she prayed, as she pulled the door to.

"There's tea in the pot," Amanda was saying. "Would you like some?"

Hannah caught a glimpse of them through the crack in the door. A thin, nervous-looking PC. He was accompanied by a girl with very dark hair. She didn't look English, didn't look like a policewoman either, apart from the uniform. She was the one doing the talking.

"Are you and Hannah close?"

"I guess."

"Would you know if she was having any … problems?"

"I suppose … look, me and my mates answered all these sorts of questions at school today."

Amanda made herself sound exasperated and upset.

"We don't know nothing and we're all dead worried about her."

Hannah smiled. Amanda was putting on an exaggerated yobbishness, trying to make herself sound stupid. Hannah hoped that she wouldn't overdo it. The WPC kept going.

"It's possible that you noticed something without realizing you noticed it. Your teachers aren't trained to ask questions. We are. So if you could just be a little patient…"

Before Amanda could reply, Hannah heard the front door opening. Amanda's mum was home.

Hannah had to get out. If she didn't leave now, she was bound to be found. She must get out this minute, while there were noises to distract the people in the kitchen.

"Amanda, are you in?"

The dining-room had French windows which opened on to the garden.

"In here, Mum. We've got visitors."

"Really? Who's…"

Hannah heard Mrs Perry coming into the kitchen, introducing herself. The key was in the lock. Hannah turned it. Then she opened the windowed doors, as quietly as she could. They squeaked a little. Hannah crept out, bag over her shoulder, pushed the doors closed again, then legged it over the lawn, leaping over the back gate which didn't open, the way she and Amanda used to when they were kids. A quick glance back – nobody looking. Another fifty yards down the lane, then she was on to the waste ground which backed on to the canal, home free.

Only Hannah had no home to go to. It was too dangerous to visit the all-night café again, now the police were looking for her. She'd have to find somewhere else...

Hannah realized that she'd left her coat behind, in Amanda's bedroom. Probably a good thing. Mum might have noticed that the coat was gone, described it to the police. But it was getting cold. She had to buy another one. The shops were open for another hour. She'd catch a bus into town. Think of it as an adventure, she told herself – you might as well – the only alternative was to think of it as a nightmare.

The bus driver glanced at Hannah's pass. That would be a dead giveaway, too, once her disappearance had been reported. Hannah looked older than she was. Bus drivers always gave her a good looking over when she held out a young person's bus pass. From now on, she'd have to pay full fare.

Outside, it was drizzling. They drove into the darkening city. Hannah knew that the moment she got off the bus, she was in danger of being spotted. She needed a coat immediately, something dull, nondescript.

There was a Barnado's opposite the bus stop in town. Hannah went straight into it. She'd never bought clothes in a charity store before. The place was full of customers. Was it always like this, she wondered, or were the people all just hiding from the rain? There were quite a few coats, priced between ten and twenty pounds. Most of them looked much too old for her. Hannah wanted to look older, but not middle-aged. She found a green anorak. It was slightly too big and too smart to be trendy – halfway between a Barbour and a Parka – but it was warm, and made her feel anonymous. It would do.

The old biddy behind the counter tried to make conversation about the weather. Hannah mumbled a reply, and handed over twelve pounds fifty. Outside, there were still a lot of people about. It was too dangerous to walk around, so Hannah went next door, to the Odeon, where there were six films playing. She chose an 18 certificate to test how old she looked. The woman issuing tickets didn't give her a second glance.

In the warm cinema, Hannah paid little attention to the film. She was too busy thinking about what to do next. If she was going to get out of town, she ought to do it quickly. By tomorrow, she expected, her picture would be in the papers. But Hannah didn't want to get out of town. She had different plans.

Later, she would get some more money out of the bank machine, buy some fish and chips and find somewhere safe to stash her bag. Meanwhile, she bought some popcorn and tried to follow the film.

It was a convoluted thriller. By the climax, it made no sense to her at all. Hannah couldn't decide whether the film was any good or not. When it was over, she stayed in her seat and watched the movie all over again, paying closer attention than before. This time, knowing how it was going to end, the plot was crystal clear. Hannah understood each twist the moment it happened.

She left halfway through. There was too big a risk of meeting someone she knew if she waited until the end. Anyway, now that she grasped the story, the film had no escapism to offer her. As she walked out into the chilly evening, Hannah wished that the complicated plot of her own life could be resolved as neatly as they'd do it in the movies. But it wasn't going to happen. Try as she might, she couldn't work out how this story would have a happy ending.

5

The shift finished at ten but everyone tended to return to the station before that, to fill in their notebooks or catch up on other paperwork. It was nine twenty. Neil Foster was still waiting for Mr Brown to arrive, so that he and Clare could interview him about his daughter. Jan Hunt was writing up the arrest of two car thieves that afternoon (they had picked up the second one at his home an hour before, eating his dinner – his mum thought he'd been at school all day). Ben Shipman was chatting to Clare about the burglary that morning. He was trying to be helpful, but not succeeding.

"If you'd IDed the white bloke, we might have a chance. The only way you'll make any progress now is by looking around the second-hand shops, seeing if any of your stuff is in them."

"Don't we know which shops take the most stolen goods?" Clare asked him. "I thought I'd look around when I'm off duty."

She was rather naive, Ben thought. She wouldn't stay that way long.

"If we knew which shops were bent, they wouldn't stay open, would they? Even when we catch the thieves red-handed, they never say who they're going to sell the stuff on to. We're talking about things being flogged in pub car parks after closing time, that sort of thing. Car boot sales – they're popular too."

"So why aren't you going there?" Clare asked.

"Not enough time. And, anyway, sorting out what's bent and what isn't, that's a tricky job. You'd need a big operation, not a couple of coppers looking around on their day off."

Clare looked depressed.

"So, basically, what you're saying is *forget it*."

"Your parents are insured, aren't they?"

"Yes, but it's not the money, it's the humiliation – a police officer, having her home burgled."

Ben laughed in a friendly way.

"You think it doesn't happen to other coppers all the time? They do what you did this morning – keep quiet about it. What else can you do? Put a sign up on your front door, saying *Thieves KEEP OUT! Police Officer's residence*? They'd probably steal everything then smash the place up for fun."

Clare didn't look amused.

"All right," Ben said. "Take a look around second-hand shops in Hyson Green, Sneinton. If you find anything, call the uniforms and give me a ring at home, too."

"What's this?" Jan Hunt asked, looking up from her typewriter. "Putting in for unpaid overtime?"

"Not exactly," Ben muttered.

He noted Clare's sour expression. She didn't like the sergeant any more than he did.

"Any word on who the new inspector is?" Clare asked.

Jan shook her head. Ben was curious about this, too. Evidently it was the new boss – not Inspector Thompson – who'd taken the decision to partner him with the winner of the working mother of the year award. As far as he could make out, Jan's mind was as much on her baby as it was on the job. He wanted to see if the decision to partner him with her was reversible. A phone rang and Ben answered it. He called to Clare and Neil.

"The girl's father's here."

"I'll get him," Neil said.

As Neil walked out of the room, Inspector Thompson came in.

"Actually," Clare told Ben, "Mr Brown's not her father. Her real father was a policeman, Michael Knight, died in a car crash five years ago."

"Mike Knight's daughter?" the boss said,

suddenly interested. "I used to work with Mike, before he transferred to CID. Great bloke. Doted on his daughter. Hannah, wasn't it? What's happened to her?"

"She's been missing since last night," Clare informed him. "No obvious reason, and it's never happened before, so we're taking the case seriously."

"What do you *think* has happened?"

"Hard to know," Clare said. "A boyfriend, probably. No evident problems at home, though we're not ruling that out, either."

"I want her found," the boss told her, in his firmest voice.

He turned to Sergeant Cope.

"Hear that? I want Mike Knight's daughter found, if it's the last case we clear up before I'm out of here. Keep me informed."

"Got it."

Ben decided that now was not a good time to ask the boss about his replacement.

Neil showed Ted Brown into the interview room. Clare sat beside him with her notebook open. She could write at twice the speed Neil could, one small advantage of working with her. All day, he'd found Clare's presence off-putting. He wasn't sure how long he could stand it. Now he tried to concentrate on the job in hand, interviewing a tired, middle-aged businessman.

"It was you who discovered that your daughter was missing, Mr Brown."

"That's right. She was late for breakfast."

"Was that unusual?"

"Hannah often skips breakfast, but she'll call that she's 'just coming' which means she'll be down in ten minutes, five if you yell at her."

"But this morning, nothing?"

"That's right. Linda called her twice. I banged on her door. No answer. Linda was getting very anxious. So I broke it down."

Clare looked up from her notes.

"Does she usually keep the door locked, Mr Brown?"

"Quite often. You know what teenage girls are like – mad keen on privacy. Linda's always on at her not to lock it when she's in bed asleep – the fire risk and all that. But she never listens."

"How would you describe your relationship with your stepdaughter, Mr Brown?"

"About average, from the way people talk about it. Teenagers – well, they're like aliens, aren't they? On another planet most of the time. But we were close. She never went short."

"She didn't resent you taking her father's place?" Neil asked, gently.

"She took my name, didn't she?" Brown replied, indignantly. "I mean, no offence to you two, but, from what Linda tells me, her real dad wasn't around all that much. And he wasn't too great a father when he was at home."

Neil decided not to bring Mike Knight into this.

"Why do you think that Hannah left home, Mr Brown?"

The man sat and thought for a few seconds.

"Like I said, teenagers … they could be from outer space half of the time. She'd been having rows with her mother…"

"What about?"

"Silly, petty things. What time she got in, drinking alcohol, the usual, I suppose…"

"But something must have spurred her to leave home. That's a big step."

"You and I know that it is, but Hannah … I'm half expecting her to walk through the door any moment. I wouldn't be surprised if she's waiting at home when I get back. But if you ask why she left in the first place…"

He put his hand to his head as though he had a headache.

"…then I'm sorry, but I haven't the slightest idea."

The interview was concluded at nine fifty. Both Neil and Clare should be getting changed now, going off duty, but the boss had said to make it a priority, so there were still some things that couldn't wait for the next day.

"She was last seen at ten," Clare said, "so, effectively, she's been gone twenty-four hours."

"I'll get the details faxed to the national computer," Neil said. "You get them sent on to the Missing Persons Bureau in London."

"You think she's gone to London?"

"It's possible," Neil said, thoughtfully. "Most runaways don't go that far. They prefer to stay around places they know, friends and all that. But I've got a feeling that this one might be different. Can you brief the night shift?"

"Sure."

It was gone ten when he'd finished. Clare was already changed. She was wearing jeans and the brown overcoat which Neil knew so well. He found himself thinking back to the summer before, when he first went out with her. He'd thought that she was getting keen on him back then, when, really, she was more interested in getting details of the investigation into her brother's death. But then it had become more than that, much more.

"Fancy a drink?" he asked her now.

"Sorry," she told him. "I'm meeting someone."

The way she said it left no doubt in Neil's mind. Clare was talking about a bloke. Neil turned away, trying to hide his jealousy. He thought of something cutting to say and turned round to say it to her. But she was already gone.

*   *   *

Clare walked into the Peacock at quarter past ten.

"Sorry I'm late."

"You look absolutely exhausted."

"It's been a long day. I'll tell you about it when I've ordered a drink."

"Got you one already. Bacardi and Coke, right?"

"Right."

Clare took a slurp. The ice had melted and the drink was a bit too watery, but it was wet and alcoholic and began to take the edge off her horrendous headache.

"I'm sorry," she said after a while. "I'm not very good company tonight. I don't want to bore you by telling you why."

"I won't be bored. What are friends for?"

"OK. If you insist."

Clare ran through the events of the day, starting with the burglary at half past three, finishing with Neil asking her out for a drink.

"He's so … persistent. How can I work with him?"

"You can't. Put in for a new partner."

Clare sighed.

"You told me to do that last time, and you were right. But I can't do it again."

"If he won't, you have to."

"I guess … let me get you a drink."

"No, I'm fine. You look dead on your feet. Why

47

don't I run you home? My car's on North Sherwood Street."

"Would you?" Clare said, gratefully. "You know, my feet are killing me. I'd forgotten what a killer it is, walking round all day."

"You're not kidding."

"Aren't you going to tell me about your patrol?"

"Another time. Look, we're both on afternoons, so why don't we turn it to our advantage? Give ourselves a couple of days to get used to the footwork, then go clubbing one night. How about Harpo's, on Wednesday?"

"Sounds good to me," Clare said, "if my feet are used to it by then."

"I know what you were like at Ryton. A couple of drinks and you'll be dancing all night."

Clare smiled. They got their coats and walked up the Mansfield Road.

"The thing is," she said, "I feel really guilty about Neil. Part of me still cares for him a lot."

"Only part?"

"If he wasn't in the job, I'd still be with him."

"We agreed," her companion replied. "Going out with coppers is a mug's game. And going out with one on the same shift as you? That would be suicide. Wait till we get to Harpo's on Wednesday, we'll have blokes throwing themselves at our feet."

"If you say so."

"I say so."

Ruth Clarke smiled, then got into her Volkswagen, opening the passenger door for Clare. Clare's friend was a small, mousy girl. It was hard to imagine blokes throwing themselves at her feet. A few years ago, her height would have barred her from entering the force. But that would have been Clare's loss, as Ruth was the closest friend she had made in her class at Ryton. And Clare was going to need a good friend to get through the next few weeks.

6

Henry had been sick in the night and Kevin was on call at the hospital, so Jan had only slept in fits and starts. Maybe, Jan thought, as she booked out a car for the day, she'd have been better off taking a desk job, or sorting out a job share with that WPC who did schools liaison. She had a small kid, too.

Jan was late in and surprised to see everybody still sitting around the parade room table, listening closely to Inspector Thompson. Sitting next to the inspector was a young, slick-looking bloke in an expensive suit. At first, Jan assumed he was a reporter. Then she looked again at the way he was dressed and decided that he was a lawyer.

"We had a couple of reports about the missing

girl, Hannah Brown, last night," the inspector said. "Someone claims to have seen her on a bus, not far from where she lives, at teatime. A parent of one of her friends thinks she might have seen her in Slab Square, at around a quarter past nine. Clothing details sketchy. It was dark. But she's a police officer's daughter and I want her found. Neil and Clare: it's your top priority. All right?"

"Yes, sir."

Thompson smiled one of his rare smiles.

"And now, for the moment you've all been waiting for … my replacement. I'd like you to meet Inspector Paul Grace, who's been transferred to us from Trent division. I'm sure you'll make him as welcome as you've made me."

There were a few restrained laughs as he said this. Thompson had never been popular. He was too irritable. But Jan felt a sudden surge of affection for the inspector as his replacement stood up. Paul Grace, with his tightly trimmed blond hair and poncy Paul Smith suit, couldn't be a day over twenty-five. He had *graduate fast track* written all over him.

"I'm sure I'll get to know you all very well over the next few weeks," Grace said, in a BBC voice. "I'll be familiarizing myself with the station's routine and asking a lot of questions."

He was young and soft, Jan decided, and talked like a personnel training manual. Why, she wondered, did I come back to the job? Who needs some bloke barely out of nappies in charge of you?

"I hope that I'll also be able to offer you all the support you need, whenever you need it. My door, as they say, is always open."

Everybody dispersed. Jan joined Ben in the car.

"Sod this for a game of soldiers," Ben said. "That bloke's hardly a day older than I am. I thought that Notts was supposed to value experience more than other forces? You're not telling me he's done anything but go to school, then university, then straight up the ranks."

Jan said nothing, agreeing with Ben for once. Grace would have done the minimum two years as a copper, passed his sergeant's exams first time, then done the two year minimum stint there before graduating to inspector. As far as she was concerned, the new inspector was bound to be wet behind the ears. But Jan was a sergeant herself. She wasn't going to slag off a superior officer who she didn't really know. Instead, she turned the question round.

"Did you apply for the graduate fast track?" she asked Ben.

"Yeah. I didn't get taken though. They only took fifty for the whole country in my year."

"Tough."

He started driving, looking thoughtful.

"Did you go to university?" he asked after a minute.

"Polytechnic. Remember them? I did Humanities."

"Politics and Economics. What d'you get?"

Funny, the way that some graduates were obsessed with the class of their degrees, as though it meant anything in the real world.

"Two:one," she told him. "You?"

"Two:two," he mumbled, sorry now that he'd asked.

Before they could discuss the subject further, a call came in.

"Burglary in progress, 22 Vicar Street."

Ben picked up the mike gratefully.

"5117 responding. We're on our way."

Hannah Brown was in Year 11 at Greencoat School, the same year that Clare's brother Angelo would have been in, had he lived. This was the first time that Clare had been back to her old school since leaving it after her GCSEs, more than four years ago. It was a weird sensation.

Clare recognized many of the teachers as they walked past her in the tired-looking, red brick building. They were on their way to the final lesson of the day. Each one glanced at Clare but none seemed to recognize her. It was as though her uniform shrouded her real identity. Or maybe they'd just forgotten. Maybe, in their job, they had to forget old faces and names in order to remember new ones.

Hannah's form teacher was Miss Thornber, who once taught Clare Geography. She blinked abstractedly as she and Neil introduced themselves, then smiled ingratiatingly.

"Of course, Clare … I was so sorry about your brother. He was a lovely young man. You know, he was in my form, too. I would have come to his funeral, but I was on holiday…"

"I understand," Clare said.

So Angelo would have known Hannah. If he was alive, she could consult him. But then, if her brother were still alive, Clare wouldn't have become a policewoman. By now, she would be a third of the way to being an architect.

"What can you tell us about Hannah?" Neil asked.

"A very bright girl, very sparky. Expected to get As. She has her moods though, gets into enormous rows with people now and then."

"Students or teachers?" Clare asked.

"Both. But she's popular. A lot of people are very upset about her disappearance."

"Were there any signs of it coming?" Neil asked.

"None. Not even in retrospect. I've had a word with all of her teachers, and none of them noticed anything unusual."

"We'd like to talk to some of her friends," Clare said. "I believe you've made arrangements…?"

"Yes. There are five people waiting for you outside the school office. The head's arranged for you to use the interview room."

The "interview room" was a poky, converted stock cupboard. Five fifteen-year-olds were sitting outside it, looking bored.

"I hope this won't take long," Clare told them. "We'll try to be finished by the end of the school day."

"Aren't you Angelo's sister?" the only boy among them asked. "Clare, isn't it?"

"That's right," Clare said. "I am. You're…?"

"Dave, Dave Carter."

"We won't keep you long, Dave."

She turned to the first girl in the line.

"Amanda, why don't you come in first?"

Amanda Perry sat down in the uncomfortable, plastic chair. A pretty, curly-haired girl, she looked more composed than she'd been when they interviewed her at home the day before.

"I told Miss Thornber you'd already seen me," she moaned.

"I know. I'm sorry to keep you out of your lessons. But we did wonder whether you'd remembered or heard anything else since we first spoke."

"Nowt," Amanda said.

"What about the other people outside? Could you tell me how close they were to Hannah?"

"Dave and her were mates, that's all. The rest of us – Kelly, Michelle and Lucy – we hang around together."

"So you'd say that you were all equally good friends?"

Amanda pouted.

"I wouldn't say anything. You'd have to ask Hannah who she got on with best."

"I wish I had the opportunity," Clare replied, dryly.

"OK," Neil told Amanda. "You can go now. But if you remember anything…"

"You'll be the first to know," Amanda told them, almost too politely.

Next, they called in Hannah's ex-boyfriend, the one who Mrs Brown had told them about. Dave Carter was tall and thin, with a narrow face and surprisingly brown eyes. Clare could see what Hannah saw in him.

"We asked to see you because…"

"I went out with her a few times. You don't have to explain."

"When did you last see her?"

"You mean outside school, on a date?"

"Yes."

"Before the summer holidays."

"How close were the two of you?" Clare asked.

"We had some laughs. It wasn't serious."

"Where did the two of you go?"

"The pictures, parties ... we went swimming once."

Neil nodded.

"And whose idea was it to split up," he asked. "Hers or yours?"

"A bit of both, really."

Clare asked the question more carefully.

"Could you describe what happened when you broke up?"

Dave looked embarrassed.

"I suppose it was more her than me, when you put it like that. You know how it is – she said that she wanted to stay just friends, which meant that she wanted to stop seeing me out of school. I said it was fine by me. Hannah's hard to keep up with."

"In what way?"

"Clever. Forever writing things: poems, stories, diaries. And popular, too. There were always other lads sniffing around her."

"Who did she go out with after you?" Clare asked.

"How should I know? *No one* was what she told me. I took her word for it." Neil, sitting next to Clare, looked a little embarrassed.

"You've no idea where or why she's gone?" Clare asked.

"I'm worried about where she is," Dave said. "We all are."

He'd avoided answering directly, but Clare let it

go. She felt fairly sure that he had no idea where Hannah was. Neil asked a few more questions about places they went to, and whether Hannah had ever talked about leaving home. Then, almost as an after-thought, he asked,

"Excuse me getting personal, but … were you and Hannah sleeping together?"

The boy looked insulted. He told Neil where to go. Then his face went red, as he realized what he'd said to a policeman. Clare tried to smooth things over.

"All we're getting at, Dave, is that Hannah might be pregnant. It could explain her reasons for running away."

The boy shook his head, face still red.

"If you knew Hannah, you'd know that she has a really good reason for whatever she does, and, any-way, she isn't stupid enough to get pregnant."

"Some people aren't stupid," Clare suggested, "just unlucky."

"If she was unlucky, she'd know what to do. And it wouldn't be running away," Dave insisted. "I'm worried about her. Either somebody's got her, or she has a very good reason for what she's doing. Are you finished now?"

"Yes," said Neil. "We're finished."

The two of them exchanged glances when the boy had gone.

"Telling the truth?" Neil asked Clare.

"I think so. Don't you?"

Neil shrugged.

"For a bloke who'd been chucked for no reason, it sounded to me like he was taking it far too well."

Clare ignored this jibe. She got up to bring the next student in, pretending that she wasn't angry. She couldn't keep working with Neil, that was for sure. Tomorrow, she'd see Inspector Grace, ask him about a new partner. She'd be quite happy to work with John Farraday or Tim Cooper, both of them experienced coppers who she could learn a lot from, given the chance.

They didn't get anything new from the other three girls. Each one confirmed that Hannah was a popular, intelligent girl whose one flaw was a bit of a temper. None of them, Clare noted, had known Hannah at primary school. They couldn't say how Hannah reacted to her father's death. Indeed, the girls seemed only dimly aware that Ted Brown wasn't her real father. At the end of the interviews, the two officers were no nearer to locating Hannah than they were when they arrived.

"Do you think any of them know anything?" Neil asked.

"I dunno," Clare replied. "Yesterday, I thought Amanda Perry looked a bit shifty, but, today, I wasn't sure. There was one thing, though, something Dave Carter said. 'She was always writing.'

Did you see much writing in her room?"

"Nothing that looked like it wasn't for school."

"If she kept a diary, it might explain why she left."

"If she kept a diary, she probably took it with her."

"Probably," Clare said. "But it's worth a look."

7

Most police work has little to do with detection. The clear up rate for the majority of reported crime is less than twenty-five per cent. When you catch someone, ninety-nine times out of a hundred, you're merely playing your part in the law of averages. It's not detection, but dumb luck.

Jan tried explaining this to Ben Shipman, but he wasn't really listening. Because, today, they got lucky.

It started with a car with a dud tail light, at half past eight. Jan was driving. She put on the siren and the blue light, but the Ford Fiesta didn't stop immediately. Then it did. Ben was about to get out of the Panda when the call about the burglary came in. The thieves had been seen leaving the house. Jan and Ben were only two minutes away from the scene of the crime.

"Forget this lot," Ben suggested, eagerly. "Let's go for it."

"The thieves are already away," Jan told him. "The sarge is out in a car. Let him take it. Why don't you handle this?"

Irritated, Ben got out of the car. Jan smiled: he'd have to learn not to keep chasing the glamour jobs, or he'd never be a really good copper. She took her time, getting the breathalyser ready in case Ben thought it was needed, watching him walk up to the Fiesta, politely asking the driver – white guy in denims, about thirty – to get out.

Despite his irritation, Ben was playing it by the book, showing the guy the tail light, politely throwing in the fact that he'd been driving faster than the legal limit (not that there was anything he and Jan could do about this. They had no way of proving it). The man in the passenger seat, meanwhile, ignored what was going on, staring straight ahead. That was the first thing which made Jan suspicious.

The call came in just as Jan was walking over to join Ben on the main road.

"Suspects are two white men in their late twenties, seen leaving the scene in a red Ford Fiesta."

Jan didn't blink. She took a step back, so that the man busy apologizing for his broken brake light wouldn't hear, then spoke to Sergeant Cope on the radio.

"4523 here, sir. We've got them. 5117 is currently interviewing the driver about a broken tail light on Robin Hood Way. Shall we arrest them now, or wait for back-up?"

There was a silence punctuated by radio crackle. The sergeant was trying to decide what to do. Jan could hear Ben asking the driver where he was going. The man gave an address in Radford. Ben was telling him to call in to Radford Road police station and produce his documents.

"We've got two cars here," the sergeant said. "Me and CID. Follow them, but at a distance, like you're keeping an eye on his speed. We'll find out where they're going."

Ben got back into the car and Jan explained the situation.

"Why didn't we just arrest them?" Ben asked, annoyed. "Didn't the sarge think we could handle it? Or does he want all the credit?"

"It's got nothing to do with credit," Jan told him, short-temperedly. "If we arrest them, we don't find out where they're taking whatever it is they've got in their boot."

"And what if we lose them?"

"We won't."

She set off. Ben didn't hide his annoyance. It was the first really interesting bit of driving they'd had and Jan was behind the wheel. She'd insisted on driving at the beginning of the shift. If Ben's style of driving irritated Jan, hers annoyed him twice as much. She was the original jerky, bash the gearbox, bobby in a battering-ram. But she managed to keep exactly a hundred yards behind the thieves, who were driving at a precise, nervous thirty miles an hour.

As the Fiesta crossed Alfreton Road, Sergeant Cope radioed Jan to let them go.

"We've got an unmarked car waiting on the other side of Radford Boulevard. Let them think they're safe."

Jan did as she was told, but turned quickly off into a side road.

"Where are we going?" Ben wanted to know.

"Woman's intuition," Jan teased him.

A minute later they were cutting across Hartley Road, ready to catch up with the thieves as they drove round the flats and into Garden Street.

"It's a warehouse," the CID officer in the unmarked car announced. "They're getting out, unlocking it."

"We're thirty seconds behind you," Jan announced. "On our way."

"We'll block their exit on to Ilkeston Road," Bill Cope said.

And then it happened: one of those moments of rare beauty. The two CID men got out of their car at the precise instant that two Pandas – lights flashing, sirens singing – blocked each end of Garden Street. The thieves, who had already unlocked the door of the warehouse, were trapped. One of them ran inside. The other ran straight into the arms of Sergeant Cope.

Jan, Ben and the two CID blokes charged into the dark warehouse. They could hear the thief, clattering through disused spinning equipment, trying to get to the fire escape. As the three men ran after him, holding their torches out, Jan took a chance. She felt along the wall, near the door. Maybe the electricity was turned off, but maybe it wasn't. She found the switches, and pulled every one of them.

Fluorescent lights flickered, then came on, dazzling the officers, who had gone off in the wrong direction, and illuminating the thief. He was caught in the centre of the warehouse, surrounded by aisle upon aisle of electrical goods, all of them second-hand and all of them, Jan would bet, stolen. She walked up to the man who, minutes before, had thought his biggest problem was a broken tail light.

"You don't have to say anything, but anything you do say…"

Later, when they had him in the interview room, the man would have a great deal to say.

When Clare got back to the station, there was something big going on. The night shift had just arrived and they were all excited by it, waiting for an arrest to come in.

"There'll be some overtime tonight," Neil said, grudgingly. "Think I'll hang around and see what the score is."

Clare was curious too, but she'd arranged to go out with Ruth and it wasn't her case. She would have to find out about it tomorrow. Actually, it was a relief that the car wasn't back, because it meant that Jan Hunt wasn't there to see her getting changed in the Ladies, swapping her black and blues for soft jeans and a silk blouse. Clare doubted that the sergeant would approve.

In the noisy nightclub, Clare could tell Ruth the details of her day with no danger of anybody over-hearing.

"Neil keeps complaining. He says that they hardly ever give any attention to runaways."

"Even if they're kids who aren't in care, who haven't run away before?"

"I think his main gripe is that he's out walking all day. Neil doesn't like the beat. Apart from this case, most of what we do all day is community liaison. Lots of cups of tea. The odd domestic."

"Sounds like my beat," Ruth told her. "You need a strong bladder. But you meet people, have a chat. If the weather's OK, I think I prefer it to being in a car all day."

"Me too," Clare said. "But not with Neil."

"So when are you going to ask for a change?"

"I don't know. Tomorrow, maybe, if the new boss is in."

"Tell me about him. What's he like?"

"Small, for a copper. Good looking, in a slimy sort of way. A greasy pole type, on his way to a cushy job at the dream factory."

The "dream factory" was Divisional Headquarters. Clare and Ruth didn't think that they'd end up there. Neither of them were graduates, for a start. Clare had dropped out of university to join the police, while Ruth used to work as a clerk and typist at a police station in Yorkshire.

Clare was about to go on about Paul Grace when they were interrupted.

"Are you dancing?"

"Are you asking?"

The two blokes standing in front of them were presentable: longish, well-kept hair, not badly dressed. The taller one focused in on Clare. She wasn't really looking for someone, except as a dancing partner. But she and Ruth exchanged glances. Ruth seemed to like the look of the other lad, with the stubbly beard, the one who now spoke.

"We're asking," he said.

The two girls stood up at the same time.

"All right," Ruth told him. "We're dancing."

Despite having been on her feet all day, Clare

found new energy on the dance floor. The music mattered more than her partner, who Clare decided she didn't fancy very much. He kept trying to make inane conversation, but Clare concentrated on the music, not telling him much about herself except for the fact that she still lived with her parents. That would stop him getting the wrong idea.

Ruth was really letting herself go. You'd never think that she was such a raver if you saw her in uniform. At work she was dowdy, bespectacled, with short hair and an unremarkable figure. But when she wanted, she could shed all of that. Tonight she had her lenses in and wore a black singlet with fluorescent leggings. She looked a lot livelier than Clare felt.

The guy Clare was dancing with (Mark, or Mike, it had been hard to hear) reached into his pocket and pulled out a small bottle. He took a sniff from it and then offered it to Clare.

"No, thanks, I don't."

"It'll help you enjoy dancing more."

"I'm enjoying it enough already."

The youth shrugged and flicked his hair away from his eyes. He leant forward conspiratorially and spoke directly into her ear.

"You know, Clare, I get the feeling that you're quite square. These are only poppers. Try it. Let go. They're not illegal, you know."

"I know," Clare said, speaking loudly into his ear.

"Which is a good thing, because, if they were, I might have to arrest you."

The lad laughed, then gave Clare a long, serious look.

"You're a policewoman," he said.

It was half a question and half a statement. Clare nodded.

"Her too?" he said, pointing at Ruth.

Clare didn't reply. The boy stopped dancing, walked over to his mate, and shouted something at him. The bearded boy looked at Clare, then looked at Ruth. Then the two of them walked off.

Ruth came over to Clare, looking more than cheesed off.

"Don't tell me," she said. "I've worked it out. First rule of dating: never tell the object of your carnal lust what you do for a living. Make up a convincing lie – like you're a student, or a brain surgeon, whatever. Will you remember that in future?"

"I'll remember that," Clare apologized.

"Come on then, dance opposite me. We might get lucky again."

The place was filling up. It was surprising how many people were able to come out late on a Wednesday. It was midnight. Clare's parents would be fast asleep, but, here, the evening was just beginning. The more Clare danced, the more she relaxed. She was young, single and she had a job.

The world looked good to her.

"Come on," Ruth said. "Let's take a break and have a drink." They headed to the bar upstairs, which was quieter. Even so, it was very busy. Despite her size, Ruth insisted on queueing to get served. Clare looked around the crowded room, curious to see if there was anybody that she knew.

Then she spotted her.

At first, Clare thought that it was a trick of the light. The girl in the pink blouse looked twenty, not fifteen. But then she looked in the direction of the bar and Clare was sure. Those eyes, that mouth which was slightly too big for her face. It was Hannah Brown.

Clare grabbed Ruth.

"Hey, I was just about to get served!"

"Quickly," Clare said, leading Ruth away from the bar. "I need your help."

"What is it?"

"My runaway girl. I'm sure that's her, over in the corner."

"You're kidding? And look who's with her."

Returning from the bar with two drinks in his hand was the bearded youth who Ruth had been dancing with earlier.

"It can't be her," Ruth went on. "You have to be twenty-one to get in here."

"I'm not," Clare replied.

"Yeah, but she's only fifteen. Come on, we're not

on duty now," Ruth said. "Leave it."

"Leave it?" Clare protested. "I've spent most of the last three days looking for that girl."

"OK." Ruth reluctantly agreed. "But this is our night out. Get on the phone. Call a uniform."

"You know how busy they are at this time of night! Suppose she goes home with Sunny Jim before they get here?"

Ruth looked frustrated.

"All right. How do you want to handle it?"

Clare shrugged.

"Go over there, get her."

"Let's do it then."

The two women walked over to the corner, pushing their way through the teeming bodies. Ruth couldn't see a thing, relying on Clare to guide her. Clare kept her eyes on Hannah. The nearer she got, the more convinced she was that she was looking at the missing girl. But she wasn't a hundred per cent sure. Why, after all, would a runaway be spending time in a nightclub in the middle of town, only a ten minute bus ride from her home? It didn't make sense.

Someone banged into Clare, spilled half an inch of beer on to her blouse.

"Sorry, gorgeous. Want me to lick it off?"

Clare swore at him. She had lost sight of Hannah for a moment. Now she saw her again, standing. The girl was looking in her direction. The bloke who danced with Ruth earlier was pointing at Clare. Then the bloke was still there, but Hannah was gone.

"She's spotted us," Clare shouted at Ruth.

"The door," Ruth replied. "She'll try to leave."

They were fast, but Hannah was faster than both of them. In the foyer, Clare asked after a brown-haired girl in a pink blouse.

"Yeah, I noticed her," the bouncer said. "She collected her coat about a minute ago."

They looked out into the dark, drizzling city streets.

"Did you see which way she went?" Ruth asked.

"Sorry, duck. Friend of yours?"

Clare shook her head.

"I don't think it's worth it," Ruth said.

Clare went to the phone in the corner, told the station that she'd seen Hannah and described what she was wearing. Then they went back to the dance floor, but the heart had gone out of the evening. As Ruth went for drinks, the bearded boy collared Clare.

"What were you after that girl for?"

"She's only fifteen," Clare said. "Did you realize that?"

"I don't give a toss. Is she in trouble, or were you getting back at me for dumping your mate?"

Clare laughed awkwardly.

"You could say that she's in a kind of trouble.

What did she tell you? It could be very helpful."

"Why should I tell you?"

"Because if you don't, I'll get someone large and unpleasant to take you back to the station and ask you the same questions."

The boy sneered.

"She didn't tell me nuffin'. She likes raves and she likes blokes with beards. Her name's Mandy and she works in a hairdresser's. She was more interested in talking about me."

"I'll bet she was," Clare said. "Are you sure you didn't arrange to meet her later?"

"Oh, sure – as if you gave me the chance. I told her you were police and she legged it."

Clare considered asking for his name and address, but decided against. He was telling the truth, she was fairly sure of that. And Hannah, or Mandy, whichever it was, had got away.

8

Inspector Grace congratulated Ben and Jan on their work the night before.

"An important find. CID are very excited by it."

"What about the stuff in there, sir? Was it all stolen?"

"Your guess is as good as mine. CID are keeping the warehouse under surveillance. The two burglars are being questioned again today. We could be on to a major fencing operation."

"Will we get a taste of the action, sir?"

Grace shrugged.

"Hard to say how it'll turn out. But you'll get your share of the credit, I'll make sure of that."

Ben smiled and went back to his paperwork. Jan remained.

"Was there something else, sergeant?"

Jan took a deep breath. There wasn't going to be a better time to say this than now, while she was in the inspector's good books.

"I was wondering, sir, about my being assigned PC Shipman's mentor."

Grace frowned.

"What about it?"

Jan made her voice a little harder, a little less polite.

"I wasn't consulted about it, sir. It's an extra responsibility which I wasn't expecting on my return from maternity leave."

"You're a sergeant," Grace said, dismissively. "You're expected to take on extra responsibilities."

"Generally, I enjoy them, sir. But PC Shipman and I have … contrasting styles. And he constantly gives me the impression that he would rather be with someone else."

"How does he give that impression? You're not implying insubordination of some kind?"

Jan felt her stomach scrunching up. She wouldn't criticize Ben, not directly.

"Not at all, sir. A personality clash, that's all."

"In police work, in any job, you have to get along with people who you wouldn't normally socialize with," Grace said, condescendingly. "Forgive me asking, Sergeant, but, this wouldn't have anything to do with PC Shipman's colour, would it?"

"No! Certainly not. It's…"

Affronted, Jan was going to say that it had more to do with her being a woman, but bit her tongue instead. The inspector smiled insincerely.

"No, I'm sure it doesn't. I'll give this some thought. In the meantime, carry on. You both seem to be doing a very good job."

Ben Shipman glanced up from the typewriter as Jan left the parade room. Had he overheard any of it? Jan wasn't bothered. Yesterday, she had got home late. Henry had been up half the night and she was exhausted already. She slumped into a chair and began filling in her own paperwork.

Neil and Clare found no diary in Hannah Brown's room: no notebooks, no writing of any kind apart from that connected with school.

"Do you know if she kept a diary?" Clare asked Mrs Brown.

"Only when she was younger. I guess she threw them out. You know, I never looked through her things, or anything like that. Hannah liked her privacy."

"Tell me," Clare went on. "Did your daughter ever go to nightclubs in town – Harpo's for example?"

"Hardly. I mean, she's far too young, isn't she?"

"A lot of girls can look older than their years."

"Oh, Hannah could do that, all right – she'd go to pubs occasionally – we'd have rows about it. But she was never out late enough for nightclubs. I can assure you of that."

"What about clothes? You weren't very certain about what Hannah took with her. Do you know if she owned a pink silk blouse?"

"Possibly. But Hannah has her own clothing allowance. It's hard for me to keep up with her entire wardrobe."

"Mistaken identity," Neil said, as they resumed their beat.

"It looked just like her," Clare told him.

"But it doesn't add up. The mother couldn't remember Hannah having any clothes like the ones the girl you saw was wearing. Lots of girls look like each other." Neil softened his voice. "You wouldn't believe how many times I've seen a girl from a way off and kept watching her, thinking it was you."

Was this a veiled insult, Clare wondered? Was he trying to tell her that she looked like lots of other girls?

"In that case," Clare countered, "why did she run away?"

"Because the bloke she was with told her that you were police. Maybe she was under age, and paranoid. Maybe she was carrying drugs, even selling them. There are countless possible explanations."

"I don't know…" Clare began, but then they

were interrupted by an elderly woman looking for a lost dog.

"Doing anything special at the weekend?" Neil asked, an hour later, as they approached the station.

"Not sure yet."

"Not seeing that bloke – the one you went to the club with last night?"

Clare hadn't told Neil who she'd been with. It wasn't his business. She wasn't trying to make him jealous – not exactly – but nor did she want him to think that he was in with a chance.

"Only … I was thinking … if you really think it was Hannah Brown last night, you know – maybe she is playing silly beggars and staying somewhere, going out to clubs at night. We could…"

"Do a tour of the nightclubs?" Clare finished for him. "Do me a favour. The one thing Hannah wouldn't do is to return to Harpo's – presuming that it was her who I saw. So, do you know how many other nightclubs there are in the city centre alone?"

"Dunno," Neil said. "I don't use them much. Five, six?"

"Nearer twenty. And there's loads more on the edges of town."

"We could do a bunch of different clubs…"

"Have you any idea how much that'd cost? I can't afford it."

"I could…"

"Leave it out, Neil. If this is a way to get me to go out with you again, it's a pathetic one."

"I was only…"

"Forget it."

Inspector Grace was leaving the station. Neil nodded and walked straight past him. Clare stopped and gave him an anxious smile.

"Can I have a word, sir?"

Grace stopped on the stairs.

"Yes, what is it?"

"It's about my mentor, Neil Foster."

"There's not a problem, is there?"

"Well, yes, sort of."

Grace sighed and looked at his watch.

"I can give you two minutes."

Clare took a deep breath and spoke.

"I was very grateful to be transferred to East division, but I think you might not be aware of my relationship with Neil … I mean PC Foster. We went out with each other for nearly a year."

"I see. When was this?"

"We split up just after my last patrol, when I returned to Ryton."

"So this … partnership is creating problems for you?"

"For both of us, sir. It's uncomfortable."

Grace furrowed his eyebrows.

"You're not saying that PC Foster is using his position to press unwanted attentions on you?"

Clare blushed. This was exactly the situation, but she wasn't going to drop Neil in it.

"Oh, no, sir. It's just that we…"

"Yes. I understand. I'm glad that this isn't a repeat of the situation with PC Price."

So he'd read her file. Clare shook her head.

"Not at all, sir. I was thinking that maybe I could work with John Farraday, or Tim Cooper…"

"I'll give it some thought. In the meantime, do your best to get on with Foster. He's a very good policeman, by all accounts. You can learn a lot from him."

"Yes, of course, I will … I mean, I do."

"Good. Good night."

Clare went up to the parade room, where Neil gave her a quizzical look. Grace had made her feel much more uncomfortable than Neil did. The new inspector was a cold one, she decided. And why couldn't Neil have gone to him? It would have been much easier for him to explain, man to man. But Neil wouldn't do anything which made him appear weak.

At home, Mum was already in bed, as usual. Dad was half asleep in an armchair, watching the end of the ten o'clock news, which he turned off as Clare walked in.

"Good day?"

"So so."

"Any news?"

He meant about their burglary. Clare shook her head. Though, as soon as she thought about it, she recalled that there had been a whisper going around, something to do with stolen goods recovered the night before, something big which was being kept quiet. But if it had linked up with her burglary, someone would have told her.

"No," she told her father. "No news."

He got up from his chair, slowly, awkwardly, showing his age, his tiredness.

"Oh well, bed for me. Good night, *teo*."

" 'night, Dad."

Clare put the TV back on and stared at the screen without deciphering the images which flickered in front of her. She needed to do something to unwind before going to bed. She wanted an early night. Tomorrow, she vowed to herself, she would go round the pawn shops, the sleazy, second-hand dives. Then she'd look in a paper and see what car boot sales were on at the weekend. No one stole from the Coppola family and got away with it.

On *Central News*, a photo of Hannah Brown flashed across the screen.

"Hannah has been missing for four nights now and her parents are very concerned. If you have any information whatsoever about her, please ring the following number…"

Clare thought about Hannah. Was that her, the other night? The more she considered it, the less likely it seemed. Where was Hannah tonight? It was cold. There was going to be a frost again. Where could she be sleeping? And why had she left home? They hadn't even begun to find out. Clare wondered if she'd ever have the answers.

9

Days when he wasn't working the early shift, Ben Shipman went for a run: tracksuit on, head down, whatever the weather. He varied the circuit according to his mood. Scenery didn't interest him. He was more bothered by the number of busy roads he had to cross, breaking his rhythm. This morning, he ran five miles. It was warm for late autumn. By the time he got back to his bedsit, he'd worked up a healthy sweat and was ready for a shower. The phone began ringing.

"Ben. It's Clare Coppola. You told me to give you a ring if this happened."

"If what happened?"

"I've found something – Angelo's computer – it was stolen from us on Sunday."

"Where are you?"

"Sneinton Market."

"OK. I'll meet you there in forty minutes."

"Can't you be any quicker? What if it gets sold?"

"I'll try for half an hour, but it depends on the buses. Wait for me outside the Market club."

Ben banged the phone down, annoyed at the interruption. Why had he told Clare to contact him in the first place? Because it was his case. Should he ring Jan? No. She wouldn't want to be bothered about work when she was off duty. What about CID? There could be a link with the operation they were running on Garden Street, but Ben didn't think so. The Coppola robbery had "small time" written all over it. And most CID officers worked nine to five on weekdays. They wouldn't want disturbing today any more than Jan would.

Ben needed a shower. But by the time he'd had one, changed and got to the bus stop, twenty minutes would have gone by. In ten minutes, he could run to Sneinton Market. He'd be a mess, but what the hell? Decision made, Ben pocketed his warrant card and left.

Ten minutes was optimistic. Ben was still tired from his earlier run. Mansfield Road hill, for a second time, took it out of him. But then he got to Mapperley Road and it was downwards all the way.

He wished he'd thought to bring a towel, though, some trunks. Then he'd be able to go into the Victoria Leisure Centre afterwards, have a shower and a swim. Maybe he could hire the towel and trunks.

Clare Coppola was standing by a phone box to the side of the Market club, trying to look inconspicuous but appearing anxious. She wore an elegant brown overcoat and looked like a student, not a policewoman. For a moment, Ben was embarrassed about his purple tracksuit, the sweat running down his brow. But this was work and, anyway, Clare wasn't his type. She saw him and smiled.

"That was quick."

"I ran."

Stating the obvious.

"Over there."

Ben mopped his brow with his tracksuit sleeve and gave the stall a good look. Mainly, the market sold vegetables and cheap clothes, but you got a few cowboys on the periphery. Stolen goods weren't unknown, but you could rarely prove anything.

"Have you called the station?"

Clare shook her head. Ben borrowed ten pence from her, went to the phone box, dialled the number, then had to wait nearly five minutes before he got the duty sergeant, who he explained the situation to. Saturdays were always busy.

"Come on, then," he told Clare as he left the box. "There'll be a car on the look-out in five minutes. I guess we can contain the situation till then."

The stallholder was in his twenties, with long, dark, greasy hair and a pock-marked face. Ben picked up the Amiga computer and glanced at Clare. She nodded. She was sure that it had been her brother's. Ben put it down again and spoke to the stallholder.

"You buying stuff like this?"

He pointed at the computer and a video beside it. The bloke shook his head.

"Not interested. Got my own sources."

Ben nodded. He knew the maths. If the bloke bought stolen goods, he'd pay ten, or at most twenty per cent of what he'd sell them for. Legitimate second-hand goods would cost him a minimum of fifty per cent of the sale price.

"Got a stallholder's licence?"

"Who's asking?"

Ben held out his warrant card. The man pulled the trader's licence out of his back pocket. It was legit. His name was Paul Smetton.

"Can you tell me the source for the goods on this stall?"

Smetton shrugged.

"I get stuff all over: the trade, car boot sales, you know…"

Ben picked up the power leads from two of the video recorders. Where the plug should have been the leads had been crudely cut.

"How'd they get into this state?"

"Don't ask me."

"But I am asking you."

Clare nodded at him. The patrol car had turned up.

"Paul Smetton, I'm arresting you for handling stolen goods. You don't have to say anything, but anything you do say…"

"Hold on!" Smetton shouted, attracting attention from other stallholders. "What evidence you got that any of this is stolen?"

Clare smiled coldly.

"This computer was taken from my house last Sunday night."

"There are millions like that."

Clare shook her head and pointed at a tiny Sonic the Hedgehog sticker on the side.

"Not with that sticker in that position. Nor – " she pulled open the battery section at the bottom – "with that serial number, which I've got written down on this guarantee certificate. Care to check it?"

Ben continued, "... may be taken down and used in evidence. Do you have anything to tell me, Mr Smetton? Like, for instance, where you obtained this computer, and the other goods on your stall."

"I told you, car boot sale."

"In the week, in November? That's an unusual car boot sale. Can you tell me which one?"

"I want my solicitor," Smetton sneered.

"I thought you might, but you'll have to wait until we get to the station."

The uniforms came over and took Smetton to the car. Ben waited with Clare until all of his stall had been cleared.

"Good morning's work," he said. "Fancy a drink in the Market club?"

Clare shook her head, which was a good thing, as Ben was beginning to suspect that he'd come out without his wallet.

"I don't like it in there," she said, as he checked his pockets. "But I'll stand you some lunch in the leisure centre. You've earned it."

She bought him coffee and a roll, then generously paid for his swim and swimwear hire.

"Going to the station?" he asked, as she left.

Clare shook her head.

"I've done enough unpaid overtime. So have you."

"I guess so."

Ben said goodbye. He'd go to the station anyway, he knew that, just to keep tabs on the case. If you wanted credit, if you wanted to move fast, you had to put in that bit extra. With Sergeant Hunt holding him back, he'd need to push himself even more.

10

Hannah went to get some money, so that she could get into another club. When you were living rough, it didn't make sense to carry much cash – you were more likely to be robbed. She'd been getting by taking out ten or twenty pounds a day. But nightclubs were expensive, even when you never bought your own drinks, and her savings wouldn't last for ever. There was a cashpoint machine just round the corner from Waterstone's which wasn't too public. Hannah darted past the Victoria Centre, and crossed at the Old Corner Pin. There were two police officers on patrol, walking towards her, so Hannah pretended to be studying the window of the Disney shop until they'd gone. Then she hurried down Clumber Street with her head down, praying that she wouldn't be spotted.

Hannah needed somewhere to stay tonight. She couldn't sneak into friends' houses and sleep there while everyone was out, not at the weekend, because there was always someone in, or likely to return. Added to that, the nights were getting longer, and colder. There was a limit to how many of them she could walk the streets, sheltering in doorways and cafes, searching for something she wasn't sure she'd recognize if she found it.

Last night, she'd got lucky. At two, Hannah wandered into a bar in Hockley, an unlicensed one, where people went to chill out after clubbing. They spent their time smoking and sipping soft drinks. There, she met Mike, and got chatting to him. She'd lied about her age, said she'd had a row with her parents and didn't want to go home. He offered her a bed for the night, no strings. And he'd meant it. Maybe he was gay, or maybe he was just a nice man. Mike was twice her age, about thirty. He had a flat in the Lace Market and a fold-up bed. He had let her sleep until midday, made her a big breakfast, and kissed her on the forehead when she said goodbye. It was unlikely that she'd be so lucky a second time.

Mike said to call her parents, try and sort things out with them, but it wasn't that simple. Hannah could go to the bar again, try and hook up with Mike once more, but it was risky. She avoided going to the same place twice. Also, her picture had been in the *Evening Post* again today. Mike could have spotted it. He wouldn't be so keen to take her in if he knew how old she really was.

When Hannah typed her number into the cash-point machine, nothing happened. For a horrible moment, she thought that it was going to swallow her card. Then the plastic card came back out and she began the whole transaction again. Maybe it was time to get out of Nottingham, Hannah thought. She'd started with a plan, but it wasn't working. Maybe she should go to London, get a job, a new identity. One thing was for sure: she couldn't go back home.

The card came out again. The green neon message read "consult your bank". Had she been too nervous, too preoccupied? Had she typed in the wrong number twice? Hannah tried to concentrate, but it was hard. She had been standing here too long a time. She would be spotted if she didn't keep moving. But if she got her number wrong a third time, the machine would definitely swallow her cash card.

The card was sucked in. Hannah typed her number, then pressed the button for "withdraw cash", then "proceed", next the amount, £20, finally "proceed" again. The machine whirred and buzzed. Hannah felt a cold trickle of fear running down her spine, the fear of being alone in the city with no money. Inside the machine, the green neon sign gave a new message. "We apologize. This machine is now empty. Please use another machine." Her card hadn't come out. Hannah wanted to hit the cashpoint, to scream, but she couldn't draw attention to herself. She was about to walk away when the message suddenly changed. Now it read: "please withdraw your card." Hannah grabbed it, nearly crying in relief.

Turning away from the hole in the wall, Hannah saw a slim youth in a bomber jacket, not that much older than she was.

"Run out of money?" he asked.

"Sort of."

He looked vaguely familiar. She remembered where from and decided that her luck was in.

"Do I know you?" the boy enquired.

"You do now," she told him.

It was nearly three when Clare and Ruth left the Hippo. They'd spent hours on the dancefloor and Clare felt more relaxed than she had done for ages. The city was quiet.

"Want to share a taxi?" she asked Ruth.

"Might as well."

They both lived in roughly the same direction. Slab Square, where the taxis went from, was a two minute walk away. As they crossed the road by the Council House, Clare glanced to the side to make sure that there was no traffic coming. Then she froze.

"Don't say anything," she told Ruth in a whisper.

"What?"

"I think they're headed for the taxi queue, like us."

"Who?"

"Those two, over there. It's Hannah, I'm sure of it."

"Oh, Clare, not again."

Clare looked around. There was never a police car about when you needed one. And the couple were catching them up. Any moment now, Hannah Brown was liable to recognize Clare. The nerve of it, Clare thought, running away, then walking around in the middle of the city at all hours. This wasn't London. Nottingham wasn't big enough for a girl her age to disappear into.

The couple stopped. For a moment, Clare thought that they were going to kiss. Maybe that was all it was. Hannah had left home for love. But then the boy looked over at Clare, a hard stare direct into her eyes. At once, Clare knew who he was, knew that he knew who she was.

"Come on!" she said to Ruth. "They've spotted us."

The two young women crossed the road. The youth said something to Hannah and she said something back. Then Hannah began to run, across the road, up Bottle Street. The youth stood there, sneering.

"Hannah!" Clare called out, feeling ridiculous. "Wait. We don't want to hurt you."

She ignored the youth. They could deal with him later. But, as Clare ran past him, he held his leg out, and she tripped over it, banging her knee on the hard pavement. Getting up, Clare could hear Hannah's footsteps receding into the night. Then she could hear Ruth, speaking to the boy.

"I'm a police officer. I'm going to arrest you for obstructing the course of justice."

Obstructing the course of justice, Clare remembered from Ryton, was a non-arrestable offence, but, a moment later, the question became academic, as Ruth made an "oof" noise. The lad had hit her. Clare looked up. He was about to hit her again.

"Stop!"

The boy gave Clare a contemptuous glance. He lifted his foot, as if about to kick her. Then there was an enormous, ear-piercing sound. The lad hesitated for a moment, then ran off, in the same direction that Hannah had taken.

The racket stopped.

"Are you all right?" Ruth asked Clare.

"I'll live. How about you?"

"Only winded."

"What was that noise?"

Ruth held up a small red capsule.

"My rape alarm. I knew it'd come in useful one of these days."

Clare smiled.

"Well, it got rid of him. Didn't bring us any help though."

Then they heard the sound of running feet. Two uniformed officers appeared from the side of the Council House, too late to be of much use. Clare told them what had happened.

"So you think that was her boyfriend?" one of them asked, as Clare finished.

"I don't know, but I do know that he's bad news, whoever he is."

"Why?"

"Because he's one of two men who burgled my house last week."

11

The early shift suited Jan. Henry woke at five anyway. She could feed him and still be at the station before six with time to spare. Ben super-keen Shipman was already there, though, and gave her a big smile, the first she could recall getting from him.

"The boss wants to see you."

"Right."

For a moment, Jan thought he meant Thompson. She hadn't gone to the farewell drink for him on Saturday night, pleading maternal duties. But Paul Grace's sombre face was waiting for her inside the inspector's office. He told her to sit down.

"I've been considering your request of last week," he said.

"Oh … good."

Jan was sorry she'd asked for Ben to be moved. After all, as far as she was concerned, he was the one creating the unfriendly atmosphere. He should have asked, not her.

"Do I understand you correctly when I say that what you object to is not the role of mentor *per se*, but PC Shipman's attitude?"

Typical Grace. *Per se*. Jan had a degree too. There was no need for him to use Latin to impress her.

"He constantly gives the impression that he'd rather not be working with me, if that's what you mean, sir?"

"And the feeling's mutual?"

"Yes."

Grace nodded and smiled condescendingly, as though he were about to do her a favour.

"I'm sorry that the arrangement didn't work out. I gave some thought to it, but, as you've demonstrated, it's difficult to deal with personnel matters when you don't actually know the personalities."

"Quite," Jan said.

"So I'm assigning Officer Shipman a new mentor."

"Good."

"And I'm assigning you a new protégé."

"Fine."

Suddenly, Jan had an uncomfortable feeling – as though she had shot herself, *metaphorically* (as Grace would put it) in the foot. The inspector lifted a phone.

"Neil, come in here, will you?"

For a moment, Jan thought that Grace was pairing her with Neil Foster again, which would suit her fine. But that didn't make sense, because Neil had already passed his probationary period.

"Neil will be taking over as mentor to PC Shipman. He'll be taking over your cases, too. Perhaps you'd be good enough to bring him up to speed."

"Yes, of course. What about…?"

"You'll be taking over Neil's tutee, PC Coppola."

Jan groaned. She'd lost Dick Tracy and drawn Nancy Drew. Jan didn't know Clare Coppola very well, but everything she did know about Clare irritated her. She bit her tongue.

"Thank you, sir."

"Don't mention it."

Bill Cope smiled at her as she came out of the office.

"Back on the streets for you, eh, Sergeant?"

Jan couldn't believe it. Four months after having a baby, they were making her go on the beat, while Ben Shipman continued to swan around in a patrol car, playing cops and robbers. Jan felt like giving up. Instead, she put on her toughest voice.

"Where is she?"

"She's yours as soon as she gets here."

Clare Coppola walked in a moment later, still tucking her blouse into her skirt.

"Where have you been?" Jan snapped at her.

Clare blinked tiredly. She didn't look like a policewoman, Jan thought, she looked like a fashion model expecting to be indulged as she arrived for an early morning shoot.

"I overslept," Clare told Jan, irritably. "I put in twelve hours overtime yesterday, sweeping the city for this missing girl."

"Don't give me excuses," Jan lectured. "Late is late."

"What's it got to do with you anyway?" Clare moaned.

Jan told her.

"I can't tell you how good it is to be behind the wheel of a car again," Neil told Ben Shipman.

"Good to be with you."

Neil smiled.

"Yeah, well ... I expect you're not too happy about losing Jan, but believe me, I couldn't have worked with Clare for another week. If she hadn't put in for another mentor, I'd have had to ask the boss for a change myself."

Ben nodded.

"Doesn't look too good on your file, though, does it?"

"You can say that again," Neil laughed. "Anyway, Jan Hunt taught me everything I know, so … what she hasn't taught you already, I'll try and fill in. All right?"

"Sounds fine to me."

They set off on patrol. Ben explained to Neil about the computer recovered at the weekend. Then he mentioned the warehouse raid.

"Do the two things link up?"

"Possibly. I mean, I'm just doing some of the leg-work. It's CID who are questioning all the suspects, trying to find out who's behind it all. But your girl-friend helped."

"Ex-girlfriend," Neil corrected. "What was in the warehouse?"

"Not a lot, as it turned out. The proceeds of a few other robberies, a load of old spinning gear. CID reckon it was a halfway house. Somebody would wait until there was enough stuff there and then move it all in one go."

"And the two blokes they've caught are still banged up?"

"That's right. No bail. We're hoping that who-ever's behind it won't realize that the warehouse cover is blown."

Neil smiled. *Cover. Blown.* Ben Shipman talked like a Hollywood thriller. But his heart was in the right place. Ben went on.

"And there's overtime in it, too. CID reckon that any pick up'll be at the weekend. I spent an extra shift yesterday staking the place out with Tim Cooper. Tim got the job because Jan wasn't in-terested, but if you are…"

Stake-outs. Now they were in a western as well.

"I'll think about it," Neil said.

Jan Hunt looked fed up. Clare remembered the run-ins she'd had with her the year before. At one point, Jan had threatened to charge Clare with imper-sonating a police officer, when all she was trying to do was to find out who had run over her brother, Angelo. Now, Clare really was a PC but Jan acted as though Clare was still pretending.

Jan shivered and put her hands in her pockets.

"So you searched the house and didn't find any diaries or notebooks?"

"Right, the second time we looked."

"You mean you didn't look the first time?"

Clare mumbled something.

"And yesterday," Jan went on, "did you find any-body at all who'd seen her?"

Clare shook her head.

"You know what the city's like on Sundays – dead. There aren't even any tourists around, this time of year."

"Whose idea was it to go out?" Jan asked, sarcastically.

God, she was a cow. Clare replied carefully.

"I rang Inspector Thompson, told him what I'd seen the night before."

"And he authorized the overtime even though he'd had his leaving do the night before?"

"Yes, well … Inspector Grace didn't officially take over until this morning."

"And Inspector Thompson was a friend of Hannah's dad. I know." Jan retorted.

They stopped walking.

"Is this the house?" Jan asked.

"Yes."

"They've got money, then. What does the step-father do?"

"He runs some kind of business."

Jan and Clare walked down the drive.

"All right. Here's what we do. First, follow the money. She's not begging, or selling herself on the streets, otherwise we'd have found her by now. It's possible that she's going home with a different bloke every night, but, from the way you describe her, I doubt it. We know what coat she's wearing, if she hasn't dumped it. But there's one crucial thing we don't know."

"What?"

"Where she's stashing her stuff during the day. She can't be walking around town with a big holdall. It'd be a dead giveaway. She's hiding it somewhere secure, probably somewhere near where you saw her the other night. Find that, and we've found her."

Jan rang the doorbell.

"I'll do the talking," she said.

Meaning: listen and learn – that was the unspoken message. Jan made Clare feel like a stupid schoolgirl.

It was nearly nine but Mrs Brown was still in her dressing-gown. She apologized for the fact. Clare thought that she looked a lot rougher than she did a week ago.

"Are you all right?" Clare asked.

"I'm not ill, no. It's just … now I haven't got Hannah to send off to school … you know."

Her breath smelt of stale alcohol.

"Has your husband gone to work?" Jan asked.

"No, he's still in bed. Do you need to talk to him?"

"It might be helpful," Jan told the washed-out mother, who returned a couple of minutes later and put some coffee on. Clare felt sorry for her. Obviously, Hannah's disappearance was hitting the family hard.

"I knew your first husband," Jan told Mrs Brown, as she washed dirty mugs in the sink. "I worked with him for a year when I was starting out. He was a very nice bloke. I was very sorry when..."

"Thank you."

"How did Hannah take it?"

Linda Brown sat down.

"Badly. She cried every day for weeks. Then she stopped even referring to him. If I brought up Mike's name, she'd change the subject. Oh, I went through all the stages: shock, guilt, grief and, finally, acceptance. But Hannah blocked it out."

"Did she get any help," Jan asked, "therapy of some kind?"

"No. When Hannah changed schools, I don't think she wanted anyone to know that she'd lost her father. And I remarried at about the same time. Hannah took Ted's name. We didn't make her. It was as though her way of coping was pretending that it didn't happen."

"I see."

Clare wondered what Jan could see. Mr Brown appeared in the doorway, dressed in a tracksuit which Clare guessed was never used for sport.

"Any news?"

Jan nodded at Clare.

"I think I saw your daughter, in the city, on Saturday night. She was accompanied by a young man, late teens, about five foot eight, with blond hair. Do you know anyone of that description?"

Ted Brown shook his head. His wife spoke anxiously.

"You saw her, but you didn't stop her?"

"I tried, believe me, but the man she was with obstructed me, and Hannah – presuming it *was* Hannah – got away."

"How did she look?"

"She seemed healthy."

Mrs Brown turned to her husband.

"Do you think that's all it is, Ted? That she's with some lad?"

Mr Brown looked deep in thought.

"I don't know, love. I just don't know."

Jan asked for, and got, a detailed description of the purple holdall which Hannah had left the house with. Then Jan asked about money.

"Did Hannah have any kind of savings account,

or cash machine card?"

"Yes. One of those special teenage accounts, since she was fourteen," Hannah's mother told them.

"Any idea how much there was in it?"

"She never went short," Ted Brown said.

"Could you find me the account details, please?"

While Mrs Brown went up to look for it, Jan asked the father some more questions.

"Your wife seems to be taking it hard."

"We both are. Linda … you know, she can't have any more children. We tried, kept going for tests but…"

He made an empty gesture with his hands.

"Runaways usually come back," Jan said, "a little older and wiser in most cases. How long they're gone often depends upon how much support they're getting." She paused to draw breath. "Can you think of anyone at all who Hannah might have hooked up with? From your work perhaps? Did she used to go there?"

Mr Brown shook his head dismissively.

"Hannah never came to the business. I've two places, both on trading estates. She wasn't interested. Liked to do all of her shopping in the city centre, did Hannah."

Mrs Brown returned.

"Here's her last statement. She must have taken

the card with her."

Jan took it.

"I'll need you to sign a form authorizing the police to get details of your daughter's bank account."

Two minutes later they were back on the street, where it was starting to rain.

"What did you think?" Clare asked Jan.

"I think you did right not to mention that the lad she was with was a burglar."

"Thanks."

"And I think that the parents know more about Hannah's leaving home than they're letting on."

"Why? What do you think it is?"

Jan shrugged.

"If I could analyse my hunches I'd be an inspector by now. You've had a week to mull things over. What do you think? Why did Hannah Brown leave home? To spend all her time in nightclubs?"

Clare took several seconds to reply.

"I really don't know," she answered eventually. "The way she was with that lad – the burglar – on Saturday night, it didn't look to me like they'd known each other long. So, I don't think she left for love. But maybe she left for freedom. Fifteen's a tough time. She'd be preparing for her GCSEs. Maybe she decided to go on a bender of some kind

– out clubbing it every night until her savings are gone."

"Maybe," Jan said. "The other night, did she look drunk to you? Or drugged?"

"Not really," Clare replied.

"It doesn't add up," Jan told her. "We're missing something. And until we find out what it is, I don't think we'll find her."

12

When you're in love with someone, and things aren't working out, it can seem like the whole world is conspiring to remind you of the fact. Every song you hear on the radio, every chance remark people make around you, every TV drama and half of the commercials in between seem to poke fun at you for loving, but not being loved back. That was the state which Clare Coppola had left Neil Foster in.

Neil could cope when she was miles and miles away, at Ryton. But then she was home and, worse, in his face, every day. Even so, despite what she'd told him, Neil had allowed himself to hope. Then she got a transfer. Now he had a new partner, and he found himself missing her, missing her so hard that it was like a constant pain in his side, burrowing deeper and deeper towards his heart.

Neil was convinced that Clare was seeing someone else. What other reason could there be for her to be out until nearly three in the morning? Oh, Clare said that she had been with "a friend", a woman from the course at Ryton, but Neil guessed that Clare's real "friend" had been left out of the story – to save either her embarrassment or his feelings.

The only way Neil could think of to regain Clare's affections was to find the thieves who'd burgled her house. After all, that was how the two of them had come together in the first place, wasn't it? He had helped to find her brother's killer. It might work again.

Ultra-violet lamps were kept in the property store at the station. The Coppolas' property had been postcoded with a security marker pen. This, together with the serial number, enabled Neil and Ben to prove conclusively that the computer recovered at the weekend had been the one which once belonged to Angelo Coppola. Now Neil and Ben were on the look-out for the stolen video, which had been similarly postcoded.

The trader who was selling Angelo's computer had been charged and held. Logically, he ought to have had the other electrical goods from the robbery, too. The man, Paul Smetton, claimed that he hadn't, but was almost certainly lying. He'd probably sold them before Clare got there. They'd question him again.

But Smetton wouldn't have bought the jewellery. You didn't sell gold rings or antique silver necklaces on market stalls or in car boot sales. Neil had photographs of Clare's mum wearing the necklace and brooch, and good drawings of the ring and the other brooch. Moreover, he now had a very good photofit of one of the thieves (without a balaclava on this time), provided by Clare and Ruth Clarke on Sunday.

At one time, police collaters regularly distributed lists of stolen goods to the appropriate second-hand dealers, but cuts and soaring crime levels had put paid to that. So Neil and Ben trawled jewellery shops, most of which were off their patch. If an urgent call came in, their response time would be lousy.

The jewellers were friendly enough. Business was slow and they were happy to pass the time of day looking at pictures of stolen jewellery. Of course, they said, they wouldn't buy goods which they guessed were stolen. By the eleventh shop, Neil and Ben were getting fed up. If the thieves had any nous, they would have shifted the stuff miles away, out of the county, for preference. But these guys were small time. Otherwise, why would they sell the computer to a tuppenyha'penny market trader?

"We used to get a lot more stolen stuff than we do these days," a jeweller in Beeston explained. "Don't know why that is. Maybe it's because we're more careful about checking the provenance of valuable items. Maybe it's the return of pawnshops. They're a lot less picky than we are. Or maybe there's another market. I don't know."

Tomorrow, Neil and Ben agreed, they would hit the pawnshops again. Inspector Grace would almost certainly complain that they were wasting valuable time trying to crack such an insignificant crime, but Bill Cope would back them up, for a while at least. If Grace put them under pressure, Neil could claim a hunch that the Coppola burglary was connected with the fencing ring which used the warehouse in Radford. It almost certainly wasn't, but no one was talking, so it might be. You never knew.

They were still in Beeston, miles off their patch, when the call came. Neil and Ben hurried back to the car. Neil let Ben drive. He was quicker, or maybe it was just that he enjoyed it more. All that blue flashing light, siren full blare, driving down the middle of the road left Neil with his stomach all twisted up. As they drove, he got the details: little girl, four years old, missing for over an hour.

This was the sort of missing person case which made Neil want to pull out all the stops. An innocent, at the mercy of a city full of vice. Not a fifteen-year-old girl like Hannah Brown, practically an adult, out clubbing every night, probably shacking up with some bloke. The city was full of Hannah Browns: the same girls came up on the missing persons list again and again, most of them in care when they weren't on the run. They could look after themselves.

Neil let Ben interview the mother. It was good practice for him. The mother was only Neil's age. She choked back tears, swearing that she'd never left her child on her own for more than a couple of seconds.

"You can't … it's not humanly possible to hold on to them every second of the day, is it?"

Ben assured her that it wasn't, that she shouldn't blame herself. The woman said "thank you", then burst into tears. The doorbell rang. Neil got up and went through to the other room to answer it.

Standing in the doorway were Clare and Jan. They weren't alone.

"We found this little mite wandering the streets,"

Clare told Neil.

"Why didn't you call it in?" Neil complained. "We've got the mother in tears through there."

"We only picked her up a minute ago," Jan chided Neil. "She was on the next road. If you'd cruised round for a couple of minutes before coming here, you'd have found her yourself."

Neil swore under his breath. Then the little girl ran through to her mother. Jan went in to explain. Ben rejoined Neil and Clare in the front room.

"Another victory for the cop on the beat," he said, sourly.

"Standard result for a missing person case," Neil added, caustically. "They tend to show up when they're good and ready. Still, at least you found this one."

"Yes," Clare told him, as Jan came back through, "we did. But if you'd got here a bit quicker, you'd have found her yourselves."

They were gone before Neil could explain what had delayed them.

"What is it?" Ben asked, as they got back into the car. "Clare getting to you?"

Neil shrugged.

"Trouble is," he opened up, "she really turns me on when she gets angry. It makes me think about what I'm missing."

"You're a masochist," Ben told him. "That's your trouble."

"Yeah," said Neil, ruefully. "Maybe you're right."

Michelle's mattress was lumpy. Maybe that was why Hannah slept fitfully. Or maybe it was because her sleeping patterns were all out of kilter. Last week, she had stayed at Amanda's twice, two days here and one at Kelly's, borrowing clean clothes from each: these were the friends whose parents all worked during the day. But then she had spent Friday night at Mike's in the Lace Market, and Saturday and Sunday in Radford, with Sean.

She had sneaked out on Sean at three in the morning. He hadn't known that she was a runaway. She had picked up enough on the street to convince him that she was homeless. Sean was a bit on the thick side – how many homeless girls spent time in nightclubs? He recognized her, though, or thought he did. She'd convinced him that he'd seen her out begging with her boyfriend and his dog. She'd let him think he had a chance with her, too, especially after he helped her to get away from the police. But Hannah was using him. He was thick, but not so thick he wouldn't work that out in a day or two.

It was no use. She couldn't get back to sleep.

There had to be a way out of the mess she was in. Often, Hannah found that writing things down helped her to sort out her mind. She got out her notebook and began to jot thoughts on to the page. Then she sorted herself out some clean underwear from Michelle's chest of drawers and took a towel from the airing cupboard. She felt the tank of the immersion heater: warmish. It'd have to do.

Hannah glanced at herself, naked, in the bathroom mirror. She had lost a bit of weight, but resisted standing on the scales to find out how much. Under the water jet, she soaped herself thoroughly, then washed her hair with Michelle's two-in-one. She didn't hear the front door opening, or the sound of feet on the stairs. The first thing she heard was a banging on the bathroom door.

"Michelle! Is that you?"

Hannah didn't reply. Leaving the shower running, she stepped out of the cubicle and reached out to push the bolt across on the door.

But she wasn't fast enough. The door opened and Hannah stood there, stark naked and dripping soapy water on to the bathroom carpet.

"Hello, Mrs Johnson," she said, sheepishly.

13

"And what did you do then?" Clare asked.

"I ... eh ... I think I said something like 'what are you doing here?'"

"And did she reply?"

"She said 'Michelle let me use her room.' So I told her to finish her shower and get dressed, then we'd talk. I went downstairs and rang her mother."

"You didn't think of calling the police at that point?"

"No. Should I have done? I'd come home from work with a migraine. I wasn't thinking too clearly. Linda Brown didn't suggest it either. She just said that she'd be straight over. She lives about fifteen minutes walk away. I was sure I'd be able to hold Hannah until then."

"What happened next?"

"When I'd finished on the phone, the shower was still running, so I left it. But when the shower was still on five minutes later, I went up to check on her. I mean, I know young women like to spend forever in the bathroom, but she'd run away from home, and I was suspicious."

"And then?" Jan prompted.

"The moment I opened the bathroom door, I heard footsteps behind me. I turned round and there was Hannah, running down the stairs. I shouted, I ran after her. But she was out of the front door and round the corner before I could get close to her. I was trying to decide what to do – whether to go after her in the car, or call the police, when Linda arrived. It was her who called you."

Clare and Jan looked at each other. They had been mere minutes away when the call came in on the radio. Hannah Brown might have run straight into them. But she hadn't.

"Was there anything left in the room?" Jan asked.

"Some patches of water. Underwear. And this."

The woman held out a spiral-bound notebook of the kind which reporters used. It was open, a few pages in. Clare and Jan read it. As they did, Hannah's mother walked into the room. She'd been driving around the neighbourhood, looking for her daughter. Clare held the notebook out to her.

"We think that your daughter might have left

something behind. Is this Hannah's handwriting?"

Linda Brown nodded. Jan took the notebook from Clare and said to Mrs Johnson, "Perhaps you could take this officer upstairs to have a look at Michelle's room, just in case you missed something."

"Of course."

When they'd gone, Jan spoke to Linda Brown.

"Can you explain what this means?"

Mrs Brown read the words. There weren't many of them.

I can't stop. If I stay

waiting to be killed.

Everything's been corrupted. What's
the point of staying and
looking?
Nothing will change, unless

Jan spoke.

"Can you explain why Hannah might feel that her life is in danger?"

Linda Brown looked blank.

"I don't … I really don't know. Hannah's very … imaginative. She would make up stories. Maybe this was one of them."

"What if it wasn't? I'm sorry, Mrs Brown, but I

think you're holding something back, something which might explain why Hannah left home."

"How can you say that?" Linda Brown complained, bitterly. "Can't you see what state I'm in? Don't you think I want my daughter back?"

"There are things I don't understand," Jan told her. "Like, for instance, why your husband was so worried about where Hannah was that he kicked her door in, but you didn't phone the police until two that afternoon."

"I explained that to the other officers…"

Jan leafed through the other pages of Hannah's notebook. She found a phone number, what looked like half a poem. No explanations.

"Recognize this?"

Mrs Brown looked at the phone number, shook her head. She was beginning to cry. Jan put her hand on top of the grieving mother's. She spoke softly.

"Are you sure there isn't anything – *anything* – that you're holding back?"

"Do you have any children, Sergeant?"

"Yes. One. A little boy."

"Then you ought to know how I feel. I haven't seen my daughter for over a week. I've been tearing my hair out. And I've just missed seeing her by two minutes at the most. Do you think I would hold back anything which might help you to find my daughter?"

The two women's eyes met. It was only intuition, Jan knew that. You could ride a hunch, but you couldn't force it to go home with you. If Jan was right, and there was something else, it was possible that Mrs Brown didn't realize it herself, that she was hiding from something, because it was too painful. Jan knew the possibilities: there were a hundred ways to abuse a child and most of them were very hard to prove, even with the full cooperation of the victim. Was that what this case was all about?

Clare returned with Mrs Johnson. She shook her head. There was nothing of use left in Michelle's room. Jan checked her watch. The shift was already over. She would have to ring Dawn, tell her that she was going to be late, again.

"We'll be wanting to talk to Michelle, and a few of her friends. If either of you think of anything which might be useful, please ring the station, leave a message for me. Can I use your phone?"

Jan rang Dawn, then the station, arranging for a car to pick them up. It would be best if someone went to Greencoat School immediately, interviewed the girls there before they had time to get their story straight. But it was unlikely that the station had enough officers to do that now. It would have to wait until tomorrow.

Sergeant Wheeler, from the afternoon shift, drove

them back to the station. Jan briefed him as they travelled.

"She's been staying out nights, staying with friends during the day. Now she can't do that any more. She'll get tired. She might make mistakes. With any luck, we'll flush her out in the next day or two."

Wheeler seemed uninterested.

"Lot of effort for a fifteen-year-old who's left home off her own bat."

"She seems to think that she's in danger," Jan told him. "How would you feel if she were your daughter?"

"If she were my daughter and I found her, I think I'd tan her backside for her."

When Neil got into work on Tuesday morning, Ben Shipman was already there.

"CID have been on to me again. You know that warehouse, on Garden Street? They reckon it's filling up. They're going to increase the surveillance until someone shows up to collect. Do you want in?"

"Maybe," Neil said. "What are the hours?"

"Twenty-four hour surveillance. Standard shifts."

Neil whistled.

"You short of money or what?"

Ben shrugged.

"I fancy the action. Anyway, I thought you were saving for a house?"

"I am, but I don't have to work every hour that God sends to get it. What were you thinking of doing – afternoons or nights?"

"Whichever suits you."

"I'll think about it."

Neil thought about it. He would like to get into the warehouse. He'd like to go through all the stuff in there, just in case any of the items stolen from Clare's was stashed there. It was unlikely, but not impossible.

The morning parade began. The sergeant started by asking Jan if she had anything on. She might be out walking most of the time, but she was a sergeant, too, and he had to defer to that. Jan told them that Hannah Brown had been sighted the day before.

"We're off to Greencoat School as soon as it opens, to interview the girls who've been hiding her. After that, we'll do our usual route, unless something comes up."

Bill Cope grunted assent. Then he added:

"I know Brian Thompson was keen on finding this lass. But she's been seen several times now, so we know she's all right. This has got legs for another day, but then I want you to put it on a back burner. All right?"

"Yes, sir."

Clare said nothing. She didn't look too chuffed.

"Neil?"

"Actually, we'd best be off out, sir. We want to do an early wake-up call on Paul Smetton, the bloke who Ben brought in at the weekend, see if we can get a line on who supplied him."

"Good luck," Clare said.

"You'll need it," the sergeant told them.

Paul Smetton lived in New Basford with his girl-friend. It was her who poked her head out of the bedroom window of their terraced house. She looked about sixteen.

"Do you know what time it is?"

Then the girl saw who it was. It took Smetton five minutes to get up and dressed, but he accompanied them to the police station without complaint. Some people didn't function too well in the early mornings. Smetton was clearly one of them. They did the usual cautions, turned on the tape recorder and Neil started on him.

"Where'd you get the computer, Paul?"

Smetton blinked and then mumbled something which sounded like "can't remember".

"Maybe you nicked it yourself?"

"I don't nick stuff."

This was true, at least in so far as the youth didn't have a criminal record.

"We'd like to believe that, Paul, but we can't if you're protecting somebody. Who're you protecting?"

Paul Smetton looked confused. Neil had heard the tape of the interview at the weekend. Smetton hadn't been pressed hard. He'd been told that he'd probably be charged with handling stolen goods. Now, however, Neil knew that Smetton was a first offender and that gave him some extra leverage. Experienced criminals never implicated other criminals. First offenders sometimes did.

"This was a robbery, Paul, with violence. A young woman, the one you saw on Saturday, was hit from behind. Did you hit her, Paul?"

"No. I swear."

"But you tried to profit from the crime, didn't you?"

"Like I said, someone brought the computer in. That's all I bought, the computer."

"How much did you pay for it?"

"A fiver."

"Funny," Neil said. "You can remember how much you paid but you can't remember who sold it to you. I think you're lying through your teeth."

"I swear…"

Neil nodded at Ben, who spoke more gently.

"Black man was it, or a white man?"

"White."

"Someone who'd sold you things before?"

"Nah. I'd remember if…"

Neil put on his most impatient voice.

"We need a name, Paul. Give us a name."

"I told you…"

Ben now, calming.

"How old? Your age? Younger?"

"Bit younger, I think."

"There must have been a name he used. It doesn't matter if you tell us. It probably won't be his real name anyway."

"No," Smetton muttered. "I don't think it was."

"What was it?"

"An Irish name, but he wasn't Irish."

"Patrick? Seamus? Sean?"

"The last one."

"Which one?"

"Sean. People called him Sean."

"Second name?"

"I don't know. Honest to God, I don't know. All he sold me was the computer. I told him it was obsolete and he said he knew, but he'd let me have it cheap."

Neil held out a photofit.

"Is this him?"

Smetton glanced at it.

"Yes. That looks like him."

Neil spoke into the microphone.

"Mr Smetton has identified a photofit made up by PCs Coppola and Clarke."

14

Michelle Johnson was a skinny, blank-faced fifteen-year-old. And she was giving nothing away.

"I told you, Hannah only stayed at my house twice. Last Wednesday and yesterday."

"Where did she stay the other times?"

"I don't know."

"What did she tell you, Michelle? Why did Hannah leave home?"

"I don't know."

Michelle began to play with the cord on her duffle bag. Clare kept going. She was only twenty, not so many years older than this girl. She ought to be able to make a connection.

"Come on, Michelle. We want to help Hannah. We know that she's in some kind of trouble. You were the last person to speak to her. What did she tell you?"

"She didn't tell me anything. There wasn't time."

"I'll tell you what," Clare said. "Go through the morning, event by event, remembering everything you can."

"I got up. I had breakfast. My mum went to work. Two minutes later, Hannah came round the back."

"Were you expecting her?"

"She'd said she might come again. I let her in. Then I had to go to school. I was late already."

"I remember being in Year Eleven, Michelle. No one gives you much hassle if you're a few minutes late for registration. You talked to Hannah. What did you talk about?"

Michelle gave a slow-burning shrug, trying to decide how little she could get away with.

"She was cold, you know. I think she'd been out half the night."

"She must have said where she was staying. You and your friends couldn't put her up over the weekend, could you?"

Michelle shook her head and mumbled something.

"Pardon?"

"I think she was staying with blokes."

"Which blokes? Men that she already knew? Or men that she met in clubs?"

"Clubs, I guess."

"What did she say about them?"

Michelle's eyeballs slid to the side of her eyes.

"She said the first one was OK but the second one was a bit creepy, that was all."

"No names?"

"No."

"What about the clubs, Michelle? Why is she spending all this time in clubs?"

"I didn't say that she was spending all her time in clubs. Just some."

"Do you and your friends go to clubs in town a lot?"

"Can't afford to."

"So why's Hannah going to them? Why's she different?"

"Dunno."

"Why did Hannah leave home, Michelle?"

The girl's voice started to become a snarl, like that of a cornered animal.

"Dunno. Look, she wouldn't tell us, all right? We asked, but she wouldn't tell us, said we wouldn't believe her if she did."

"You said *we*, Michelle. Who else is *we*?"

Amanda Perry was embarrassed to be brought back for more questions. She quickly admitted that Hannah had spent two days at her house. She seemed to talk too much, as though keen to make amends for having lied to Clare the week before.

"I got the impression that Hannah leaving home had something to do with her family – I mean, what else could it be? – but Hannah never explained. She said it was only for a week or two."

"Is there anything else?"

"Not really. The second time, I offered to lend her some money, but she said she had enough."

This was true. Jan had discovered that Hannah had nearly three hundred pounds in her account. She'd already spent over a hundred.

"Do you know where she got her money from?" Jan asked.

"Her parents have got money, haven't they? She didn't need a Saturday job. The one she had she packed in after three weeks."

Clare didn't remember hearing anything about a Saturday job.

"Where was that?"

"Her dad's shop, or something. She didn't talk about it."

When Amanda had gone, Jan and Clare compared notes.

"The Saturday job," Jan said. "No one's mentioned that before."

"If it only lasted for three weeks…"

"Didn't her father say that she wasn't interested in the business?"

"Maybe Amanda got it wrong."

*　*　*

"That's right," Hannah's friend Kelly told them. "She worked in her dad's superstore for a couple of weeks."

"She didn't like the job?"

"The first week, she said it was a laugh. Then, next time I asked her about it, she said she'd finished."

"Why?"

"She didn't say."

"Didn't or wouldn't?"

"Hannah's … you know … touchy. If she wants to tell you something, she tells you. But she's got this way of closing conversations down… Anyway, she started getting gloomy after that."

"How long ago are we talking about here?"

"Not long. Three, four weeks ago."

By the time they'd finished with the three girls, all that Clare had learnt was that Hannah Brown had spent two or three weeks working behind the counter in one of her father's businesses. It wasn't a lot. On their beat, later, they called in on Hannah's mother, who confirmed the story.

"Hannah wanted a job, so I rang Gary, the manager, asked if he had anything."

"Why was it you who rang and not your husband?"

"Ted was in Europe, on business. In fact, when

he got back, he wasn't too pleased about the job. Said no daughter of his needed to work behind a counter for pin money. He increased Hannah's allowance and she gave the job up. I don't think she was too bothered. Hannah gets bored very easily. Have you heard anything?"

"Not yet," Jan admitted. "You'll be the first to know."

The phone number in Hannah's notebook turned out to be a flat in St Mary's Place, in the old Lace Market part of the city centre. Clare rang it twice and got a male voice on an answering machine.

"They're nice flats, those," Jan said. "I can't see that blond burglar living in one of them, can you?"

"Someone else then," Clare suggested. "It's convenient for the clubs. Think she's staying there?"

"Maybe at the weekend," Jan replied. "But if she could go back, why would she stay out cold nights, then visit her friends?"

"Maybe she's keeping it in reserve," Clare suggested. "Now that she can't risk involving her friends, maybe she'll go there."

"She left the phone number behind. How will she contact him?"

"Presumably she's been there before, so she could turn up at the door."

* * *

Back at the station, Neil and Ben were hurrying off, still in uniform.

"A bit of overtime," Neil explained to Clare. "But we got a name for one of your burglars – Sean."

"Is that all?"

"That's all."

The sergeant shook his head when Jan suggested someone paying a visit to the flat in the Lace Market.

"Perhaps you'd like us to stake out all the houses of the girls she stayed with, just in case she returns? I'm sorry, Jan, but I warned you – this goes on to a back burner. The girl's not in any danger. She's Miss Nottingham Night Life. It's a low priority."

"She seems to think that she's in danger," Clare protested.

"Some scribble in a notebook? It's not enough."

They left it.

"I'll go round there myself," Clare told Jan as they changed back into their ordinary clothes in the Ladies.

"On your own?"

"Why not? You know, I'm beginning to think that what Neil told me was right. Hannah will be found when she wants to be found. Even if we picked her up, took her home, she could abscond the next day. Loads of girls do. What I want to know is – why is

Hannah doing it? That's all. I want to ask her, face to face."

Clare tried the flat in St Mary's Place as she went through town on her way home. The name plate by the doorbell was interesting. *Dr M. Butler*. Maybe Hannah hadn't been staying there, after all. Maybe this Butler was Hannah's doctor. But how many people had their doctor's home phone number? Clare rang the bell several times. There was no response. She went for the bus.

When she told Mum and Dad that she was going out again, they were incredulous.

"I thought the idea was early nights while you're on the early shift?"

"There's somebody I have to see."

"Your friend, Ruth?" Mum asked. "Or is it Neil?"

Clare didn't have very many friends in Nottingham. She had let some friendships slide when she went off to university, and most of the friends she'd kept were now at university themselves.

"How is Neil?" Dad asked.

Both of her parents liked Clare's ex-boyfriend, even though they hadn't wanted their daughter to follow him into the same job.

"He's busy," Clare told them. "Putting in a lot of overtime."

Only he's getting paid for his, she added silently.

*   *   *

Nothing. Nada. Zilch. Waiting in the warehouse was about as exciting as watching washing spin around in a machine. Neil couldn't believe that he had signed up for three extra eight-hour shifts this week. He liked Ben Shipman well enough, but spending sixteen hours a day cooped up with any person was liable to send you climbing the walls to get away from them.

They'd spent the first hour and a bit, while it was still light, going over the property stored in the warehouse with a UV detector. They'd come up with quite a few postcodes, none of them the Coppola's. Doubtless CID had checked all this stuff already and made sure that it was stolen property, but Neil wanted to know for himself, and Ben had helped.

"Aren't you clutching at straws?" Ben asked him. "I mean, even if you track down whoever burgled Clare's house, it doesn't mean that she's going to start going out with you again, does it?"

"But maybe she'll respect me more. That'd be a start."

"What is there to say that she doesn't respect you at the moment? I thought she told you that it was the job, that she didn't want to go out with another copper?"

Neil crouched on an upturned tea chest, thinking.

"That's just a line, isn't it? If she liked me enough, she wouldn't care what job I do."

"I don't know," Ben told him. "I mean, how many cop marriages do you know about? Hardly any. It's too much stress. Affairs, sure. And the women tend to be the ones who get treated badly, who get a reputation."

"I never treated her badly."

"I didn't say that. I was just saying that ... well, I can see her point of view."

"Yeah, sure, I know," Neil complained. "You've been to university, you can see everybody's point of view."

"Listen!" Ben whispered.

It was a noise all right. Neil felt in the dark for his torch. They were under strict instructions. If the visitors were depositing stuff, collar them. But if they were taking it away, radio it in, and have them followed, find where the final destination was.

There it was again. A scuttling noise. It was coming from the corner, where Neil and Ben had been eating their sandwiches a few minutes earlier. Suddenly, Ben shone his torch at it.

The rat blinked in the light, then hurtled away, back to the hole it had come out from, a few crumbs in its mouth. The two men looked at each other ruefully, then settled in for the rest of their long wait.

15

The voice on the intercom was warm, sophisticated.

"Yes?"

"Police. I need to ask you a few questions."

The buzzer went and Clare climbed the steps to the flat.

"You don't look like the police."

But he looked like a doctor. Late twenties, tall, hair starting to recede in a distinguished way, stylish sweater and stonewashed denim jeans. Clare reached into her pocket.

"Here."

She passed him her warrant card.

"Have a seat eh … do I call you 'officer' or…?"

" 'Clare' will do fine, doctor."

"The name's Mike. What can I do for you, Clare?"

She looked around her. If she were to move into a flat of her own, this would be the kind of place she wanted: a big room, tastefully decorated in pastel colours, big splashy paintings, lots of pine bookshelves on one side. There was no sign of Hannah Brown though, nothing to indicate that she had spent any time here.

Clare took the warrant card back and held out a photo of Hannah Brown.

"I'm looking for this girl."

Mike Butler took the photo from Clare.

"Do you know her?"

Mike nodded.

"Yes. Her name's Hannah. She's a ... an acquaintance. What's she done?"

"Run away from home."

"So she told me. Is that a crime?"

"No, but it is very worrying. She's only fifteen years old."

Mike began to look a little guilty.

"She told me she was seventeen," he said. "She looked at least that old."

"Some girls do. Her picture's been in the paper twice. Did you miss it?"

"I don't have time to read newspapers."

"Where did you meet her?"

"At the Corner bar, two minutes walk away. It was late on Saturday ... that is, early on Sunday morning. She was in there on her own. I got talking to her and it quickly came out that she'd left home, that she had nowhere to stay that night."

"And then…?"

Mike pointed to the couch.

"That turns into a bed. I offered it to her for the night. That was all – I'm not interested in teen-agers, whether they're fifteen or seventeen. I made her some Ovaltine, advised her to make it up with her parents, and gave her my phone number in case she needed help in the future."

The story was smooth, Clare thought – almost too smooth.

"What time did she leave?"

"I was meeting some friends in the Park for lunch on Sunday. I offered to give her a lift somewhere, but she took off on her own."

"Did she have a bag with her?"

"Yes. She picked it up when we left the Corner bar, a big purple thing."

"Where had she hidden it?"

"Behind a bin just down the street."

"Can you show me?"

"If you like."

Mike Butler looked at his watch.

"I'm meant to be meeting someone for a drink. Care to join me?"

Clare thought for a moment. The doctor was suave, good looking. He was probably meeting his girlfriend. But she hadn't finished asking him questions and a pub would make a more relaxing atmosphere.

"Just a quick one," she said. "I'm on earlies tomorrow."

"So am I."

As she put her coat back on, Clare thought of asking what a place like this cost, but there was no point – she knew that she wouldn't be able to afford it on a policewoman's pay.

Mike pointed out the bin on their way to the County Tavern. There was no bag there.

"She's probably got places all over the city where she can stash it," Mike suggested.

The pub was crowded and noisy.

"No sign of your friend?" Clare asked, as Mike returned from the bar with their drinks.

"No. It was only a casual arrangement."

Mike waved hello to someone at the other side of the bar, then spoke in a lower voice.

"I want you to understand that I'm not in the habit of picking up teenage girls and giving them a bed for the night. But Hannah looked scared. I wanted to help her."

"It sounds like you did the right thing," Clare told him. "I'm worried about her, too. That's why I'm here."

"I'm impressed," Mike told Clare, leaning forward towards her. "I thought that runaway teenagers were ten a penny. Yet here you are working overtime on Hannah. Why so keen?"

Clare shrugged.

"Because I'm new at this. Or maybe because Hannah was at school with my brother."

"She was his girlfriend?"

Clare explained as briefly as she could about Angelo, about how his death had led to her joining the police force. Mike was easy to talk to. Hannah must have found the same thing. Clare found herself beginning to trust the doctor, despite his silver-tongued manner. When he'd finished making sympathetic noises, she turned the conversation back to Hannah.

"Did she give you any hint," Clare probed, "as to why she left home?"

"You mean you don't know?"

"We've got less idea now than when we started."

Mike sipped his drink thoughtfully.

"I did ask, but she kept saying that she didn't want me to get involved. I suppose I assumed..."

"What did you assume?"

Mike frowned.

"She was on her own, so I assumed that it wasn't a boy. I thought that it must be some kind of abuse, physical or sexual, from someone in the house."

"Why?"

"There you've got me."

"Did she have any injuries, scars?"

"Not that I saw. But the second time, when I asked her, she said something cryptic, I can't remember the exact words, something like *it's worse than you think*. She wouldn't elaborate on it."

Clare sipped the last of her drink, thinking about what he'd told her.

"Just now, you said 'the second time, I asked her'. What did you mean by that?"

"What I said. She came to see me again."

Clare's eyes popped wide open.

"Why didn't you tell me earlier?"

"Because you didn't ask, and because you'd just told me that she was only fifteen. Doctors aren't supposed to pick up fifteen-year-old girls in clubs. It wasn't like that, but it could be made to look that way. Also, something tells me that the last thing Hannah needs right now is to be picked up off the street and returned to her parents. But I trust you. Maybe Hannah would too."

"Tell me what happened."

Their glasses were both empty, but Clare didn't want to interrupt the conversation by buying another drink.

"Two minutes after I got in last night, the buzzer went. It was Hannah. I think she'd been hanging around, waiting for me to come home. She was very cold, coughing … I was worried about her health."

Clare explained about Hannah's escape from the shower earlier in the day.

"Anyway, I couldn't get much sense out of her. She made the comment I told you about earlier, but wouldn't explain further. I put her to bed. She was still flat out when I left in the morning."

"You didn't speak to her again?"

"No. I was very tired myself. But I did do something else, before I went to work in the morning."

"What?"

"I left her a note, telling her to help herself to breakfast. Then I left her my spare key, told her to use it if she needed to."

"That was very generous of you," Clare said, meaning it.

"It was an impulse. She looked very vulnerable there, asleep on the sofa bed. Anyway, that was the reason I wanted to get you out of the flat just now. I didn't want Hannah turning up and finding you there. I think she'd have panicked and run. The thing is, she arrived about this time last night."

They had another drink, giving Hannah time to turn up. They had a lot in common, Clare found, and they continued chatting until it was gone eleven. Clare was tired and she'd missed the last bus. Deliberately.

"Come back," Mike said. "I'll make you a coffee and call a taxi."

"What if Hannah turns up?"

"If she's going to come, she'll have arrived by now. You can talk to her. It sounds to me like it's high time the two of you were formally introduced."

Clare let Mike take her arm as they made the short walk back to his flat.

Hannah wasn't there. At least this meant that Clare got more time to get to know Mike better. However, the taxi came far too quickly for her liking. She gave Mike her phone number, work and home.

"If she turns up, call me, anytime. I want to help her."

"I know you do," he told her. "But do me a favour, too. Can I call you even if Hannah doesn't show up?"

"Yes," Clare said. "I'd like that."

They stood in his doorway, faces lit up by the moon. He kissed her softly on the cheek.

"Good night, Clare."

"G'night."

From farther down the balcony, Hannah watched Mike kissing the policewoman good night. She should have known. She'd thought that he was the one person left who could help her, but she was wrong. He was an adult. He was on the other side. If she went to his flat again, the police would be there within seconds.

Hannah suppressed a cough and waited until the policewoman was gone. Then she walked back into the city streets. She knew where there was a large cardboard box which she could curl up in, maybe snatch a little sleep before morning. She coughed chestily and walked off into the night. It began to rain.

16

"And you're seeing him again?" Jan asked.

"I told him he could call me."

Jan concentrated on driving as she decided how to phrase the next question.

"You're sure that the two nights Mike Butler spent with Hannah were innocent?"

"Of course I'm sure. He's a doctor. He helped her. He told me he wasn't interested in teenage girls."

"And how old are you?" Jan asked, in a neutral tone.

"Twenty."

"Ah."

Jan decided to shut up. Clare seemed to have forgotten that Jan lived with a hospital doctor herself.

She could have warned her: the combination of a police officer's shifts and a doctor's shifts was an awkward one. You might understand your partner's situation better than someone with a nine to five job, but you saw each other less.

"Here we are. Remember, when you write this up, we're supposed to be investigating a hunch about stolen goods, not checking up on Hannah."

"What do you think I am," Clare asked, "stupid?"

Not stupid, Jan thought, just wilful and impulsive. She wondered why she'd let herself be talked into this wild goose chase. They pulled up in the Trading Estate's car park, at the side of the Bonanza Electrical Superstore.

The store owner wasn't there, so they talked to the manager, Gary Beavis, a slick-looking young man in a wide-lapelled suit.

"Yes, I remember Hannah. Nice girl. She worked here three Saturdays, behind the till."

"How did she do?"

"Oh, she was very sharp. No complaints about her work. In fact, we even commended her, on the third Saturday, when she spotted a stolen credit card."

"Really?" Clare asked. "How did that happen?"

"It's standard procedure, but few of our sales staff do much about it. If we spot a customer signing awkwardly, or acting suspiciously in some other way, we take the card away and ring it through, just as a precaution, even if the amount being spent is below our floor limit. In this case, the lad who'd handed the card over ran off. In fact, the card hadn't been reported stolen at that stage, so he'd have got away with it if he'd kept his nerve."

"Did you know that she'd run away from home?" Jan asked.

"It was in the paper, yes."

"But she hasn't been here?"

"This is the last place she'd come."

"Mind if I have a quick look round?" Clare asked. "Ask your staff one or two questions about Hannah?"

"Be my guest."

He turned to Jan.

"How long's she been gone?"

"Nine days now. Didn't Mr Brown mention it to you?"

"He keeps himself pretty much to himself, Ted does."

"How long's he had this store?"

"Three years. He started out with the MegaMart, on Palm Street, dealing in second-hand tellies and videos. Then he widened his customer base with this place."

Jan looked around her.

"Business seems good. What's the appeal?"

Beavis shrugged.

"We're cheap. New and second-hand electrical goods, guaranteed, unbeatable prices."

"How do you manage it?" Jan asked.

"The boss buys in bulk. It's all end-of-the-line stuff which the manufacturers are unloading."

"And the second-hand stuff?"

"That mostly comes from rental chains off-loading out of date models. And some trade-ins, too, particularly at the hi-fi end."

"Do you have any problems with people trying to trade stolen goods?"

Beavis smiled.

"Nah. We've had the odd, you know, dodgy bit of merchandise come through, but thieves want money and we don't buy, we only part-exchange. So it doesn't happen very often."

"Did you get anything?" Jan asked Clare in the car.

She shook her head.

"None of them know Ted Brown very well. And hardly anybody remembers Hannah. You?"

"Seems like a dead end," Jan agreed.

They drove off. Clare seemed grateful that Jan had stuck her neck out for her. In sharp contrast to Ben, she even asked after Henry. Jan gave her a detailed reply, after which Clare became thoughtful.

"Did you mean to have him?" she asked, after a while.

Jan shook her head.

"Not so soon. I'd only just made sergeant."

"When Neil told me you were pregnant, last year, he assumed that you wouldn't be back."

"I can think of people who'd prefer it if I hadn't returned."

"Was Ben one of them?"

Jan gave Clare a sideways glance.

"Not from anything he said, but he looked at me oddly sometimes. Like, when I returned from the phone from checking with my child-minder, he made me feel like I was wasting police time."

Clare laughed awkwardly.

"How about you?" Jan challenged her.

"What?"

"Do you think I should have come back full time?"

Clare thought for a moment.

"It's your decision," she told Jan. "No one should be able to stop you coming back at the same rank."

"But you don't agree with my doing it."

"I didn't say that."

"And you wouldn't tell me if you did think that?"

"No," Clare admitted. "I probably wouldn't."

There was nothing else for it. Hannah couldn't involve her friends any further, not after what had happened on Monday. Mike's was the only place left. She'd watched him leave for work. The moment his car was out of sight, she let herself into his flat. It was warm, gloriously warm. She sank into an armchair.

When she woke, hours later, the heating was off and the flat was no longer so warm. She went to the kitchen and made herself some toast and coffee. It was only as she took it through to the living room to eat that she noticed the note, propped up on top of the television. Her name was written across it.

It was true what they said about doctors' handwriting. The note was short and simple, but she had trouble making out all the words.

Hannah,
Last night I met a police woman who's looking for you. The police are very concerned about your safety, as am I, and she'd like to help. No-one wants you to return to a situation where you're in some kind of danger, but we can't help unless you tell us what the danger is. _Please_ stay and talk to me, or if you can't, take the W.P.C.'s phone no. and call her when you're ready.
Take care,
        Mike

Underneath were written two phone numbers – home and work – and a name: Clare Coppola.

Hannah sat down, trying to decide what to do. It was tempting to stay here. Two nights before, she had half decided to tell Mike everything. It was too big a burden to carry round all the time. But what if he didn't believe her? She had no evidence, nothing substantial. She needed witnesses, photographs. She had nothing.

Hannah stuffed the note into her pocket, finished her breakfast, then went for a wash. After that, her head was clearer. You couldn't trust adults. They thought that anyone under sixteen was still a child, a hysterical child who made things up. Wasn't that what her stepfather had called her?

But she'd show them, if it was the last thing she did.

Which, of course, it might well be.

17

The restaurant was small and classy. There were fresh freesias on each table. The waiter obviously knew Mike, treated the doctor like he was a valued customer and a connoisseur. Clare hadn't meant to, but found herself letting Mike order for her.

"She came again," Mike told Clare, after saying how elegant her black, woollen dress looked on her. "The very next day. Wednesday."

"Why didn't you call me? That was three *days* ago."

"There wouldn't have been any point," Mike said, calmly. "When I got home, she'd gone. I'd left her a note, with your phone number on it. She took the note too."

"I guess that's something," Clare murmured.

The waiter brought their first course. *Gravalax*: smoked salmon with some kind of fancy sauce.

"Do you eat out much?" Mike asked her, as he squeezed lemon on to his.

"Not a lot. Student grant, you know. And my last boyfriend was more of a pizza and pub bloke."

"Another student?"

"No. He was in the job."

"Aah."

Mike changed the subject. He was sophisticated, Clare thought, sensitive. Good looking, too, though she didn't go a bomb on receding hairlines. There was a lot to be said for older guys.

"What are you going to do about Hannah now?"

"If she doesn't show up, or get into some kind of trouble, nothing. She's sixteen in January, entitled to be on the streets, if that's where she wants to be. Technically, she should stay at school until Easter. But that's the school attendance officer's problem, not ours."

"You're getting cynical," Mike told Clare, refilling her glass. "What about the mission to find her that you had last week?"

Clare shrugged.

"This week, I've had two battered wives and a three-year-old girl in a week-old nappy, nearly starving to death while her mother spent the child allowance on crack cocaine. If you let every case get under your skin, then, pretty soon, you stop getting any sleep at all."

"Point taken," Mike said. "I try to leave the hospital behind when I'm out on a Saturday night too. But I've met Hannah. I like her. She deserves to be rescued."

"Rescued from what?" Clare asked. "Why can't she save herself?"

The next course arrived and they moved on to a more pleasant topic.

It was Saturday night and it was raining. Hannah had been gone from home for nearly two weeks now. She washed and changed in the changing-room of a leisure centre which stayed open late. It was getting harder and harder to look presentable, never mind glamorous, when you spent every night sleeping in corners, outside.

The night before, she'd bedded down on Palm Street, in the unlit doorway of an industrial unit near her stepfather's MegaMart. Time was running out. Her luck could only hold for so long. Then she would be picked up by the police, taken home. More than half of her money was gone. If she was to go to London, make a new start, then she ought to do it now, while she still had some left.

Tonight, she didn't go into the city itself. It felt too dangerous, and she didn't want to risk running into Sean, who she'd spent two nights with the week before. He'd have it in for her and, anyway, it was time to try somewhere new.

In a pub toilet, Hannah washed and made up her face. Dark mascara made her bear little resemblance to the girl in the media photographs. None of the other women using the loo gave her a second glance.

The Skyy club was on Alfreton Road, by a bus stop. Hannah treated herself to a curry from the Bombay Bicycle Shop, next door, and asked behind the counter what kind of night it would be at the club.

"Busy. Saturday's the one good night they have."

"What sort of people go? Students?"

"No. Not on Saturday. Local. And, you know, people from Bulwell, Basford, on the bus route. It's cheaper than the places in town. But it's not for you, my beauty. No one really young. I don't get off until two. Otherwise..."

She smiled. The guy could have no idea how many chat-up lines she'd heard in the last fortnight, how cold they left her. Hannah went for a walk. It was too early to go to the club yet. She wished that she could call a friend, have a chat, go on the man-hunt together. It wasn't the cold which was getting to her — although she had developed a hacking cough — it was the loneliness.

Mike invited her back for "coffee", but Clare took

the last bus home. She was in no hurry to fall head-long into another relationship, no matter how nice the guy. He'd seemed disappointed, having refused to let her pay for half of the meal. Still, if he thought that that entitled him to anything, he was wrong. Clare was genuinely tired. When Mike asked her about next weekend, she'd told him (truthfully) that she was working. Not only that but, for the next seven days, she was on nights.

"Will you call me?" he asked, sounding almost urgent.

"Sure. The week after next."

It was a long time since she'd caught the last bus home, with its mixture of drunks and well-dressed strays. They were people who'd gone for a night out but lost their energy, been stood up, or simply run out of money. A few got off at her stop. Maybe they were going to the Skyy club, which was right by it. Clare didn't care. She was for an early night and plenty of sleep, to help her get through the week of long nights which began tomorrow at ten.

"How was it, love?" Mum asked.

"Nice."

Dutifully, Clare described each course they'd eaten.

"Are you seeing him again?"

"I expect so. He seems quite keen."

"So," said Dad, "my daughter's going out with a doctor, eh?"

"I'm not *going out* with him," Clare said. "I'm seeing him. That's all." Next thing she knew, they'd be asking if he was a Catholic. Sometimes, Clare thought that it was time for her to move away from home.

The club was dark, kind of old-fashioned. The guy Hannah wanted was immersed in conversation a lot of the time. Hannah could make out snatches of shouting as one record faded and another began. At first, she wasn't sure that he'd noticed her or, if he had, that he fancied her in the slightest. He must be ten years older than she was. Maybe he was with someone but, if so, she wasn't around now.

Hannah danced with a couple of other guys, swirling nearer and nearer the place where he stood. He was chatting with his mates, maybe doing some business. Once or twice, out of the corner of her eye, she thought she sensed him giving her some attention, but it could have been a trick of the light.

After an hour, she went to the Ladies to freshen up. If her make-up wasn't perfect, Hannah looked her age, or thought she did. When she came out, her prey was no longer in the corner. Instinctively, she glanced around, worried that he'd copped off and left the club. Then she was startled by a voice.

"I know you, don't I?"

Hannah turned around and he was standing right next to her. Close up, he looked a little younger. He had long, curly, brown hair and was tanned, unconvincingly, as though he used a sun lamp at a health club. He wasn't what Hannah would call very good looking, but he certainly thought that he was.

"I've seen you around," Hannah said.

"I'm Greg," the man said.

"Mandy."

The name had worked for her before. Why not now?

"What are you drinking, Mandy?"

She told him. He looked around and, almost magically, a table became free. Hannah sat down, then watched as Greg went to the bar. She took in the jealous glances of two women who Greg had been chatting to earlier. It would be just her luck if one of them recognized her. But the papers had shown a kid. Tonight, in the dark, she was a young woman.

They danced and talked. Hannah struggled with the conversation, beginning to feel out of her depth. But Greg didn't seem to notice. He kept drinking and she encouraged him, listening to him boast about his exploits, getting less and less discreet. But the drink was getting to her head, too, and his hands were all over her. She necked with him, trying to seem enthusiastic, but hating the beery, smoky taste.

"Have you got a place?" Greg asked, after putting his tongue down her ear.

"No. I live at home. My parents would go barmy if I brought you back."

She told him that she was eighteen and from Bulwell.

"I don't have to go home, though," she went on. "I could tell them I stayed at a mate's. Can't we go to yours?"

Greg was evasive. He must be married, Hannah realized, or living with someone. Maybe this was for the best, she decided. Greg's sexual advances would be harder to fend off than Sean's had been.

Without answering, he got up and went to the loo. The place was thinning out. Hannah thought about slipping away. She'd found a church earlier, with its doors open. She could sleep in there, as long as she was out before the first service. But she was reluctant to let Greg leave, not until she'd found out...

"Let's go."

Hannah looked up. Greg was standing there, with a wide grin on his face. He was dangling a bunch of keys.

"I got these off a mate. It's nowt special, but there's a mattress, bedding. It'll do us."

Hannah smiled, trying to show willing. Inside, she was scared and looking for a way out.

"What is it?" she asked. "A flat?"

"More a sort of warehouse. There's an electric fire, though. Come on."

Hannah got up, collected her coat, wondering whether her bag would be safe until tomorrow in the alley where she'd hidden it. She watched as Greg nodded at someone, presumably the person who'd given him the keys. The bloke gave them both a lascivious smile and stuck his thumb up. The whole thing felt incredibly seedy.

Greg's car was in the car park outside. He'd had far too much to drink but he was ten years older than she was and Hannah was too intimidated to insist that he leave the keys, call a taxi. She got in, wondering what she was letting herself in for. Greg put his arm around her.

"You're all right, you are, duck."

This was, Hannah realized, meant to be a compliment. She felt like being sick, but wasn't. *This is my last chance*, she reminded herself. Greg's hands began wandering. Hannah felt her flesh crawl. She had never felt more alone.

18

Sunday night. It was Clare's first night shift on this patrol.

"Jan's not coming in," Sergeant Cope told Clare as she arrived. "Baby's got a cold or something. She has to stay with him. You go out with Ben tonight."

"Fine."

Clare was sure that her Detective Training Officer would never sanction her being partnered with an officer still in his probationary period. But so what? She had passed her initial assessment in an interview the week before. Being out with Ben didn't bother her.

"Where's Neil?" she asked, once they were settled in the car.

"He's still staking out this warehouse full of stolen goods."

"I thought you were on that with him?"

Ben shrugged.

"I was. But the operation was costing too much in overtime, having three two-man shifts on every twenty-four hours. So they've dropped the overtime. Instead, they're borrowing a few bodies. Neil drew the short straw. Count yourself lucky it can't be you, not yet."

"What's it like in the warehouse?" Clare asked.

"Cold. Boring."

"Dangerous?"

"Not really. Whatever happens, he's under instructions not to get involved, but to radio it in, let someone else make the decision. If you ask me, it'd be a lot cheaper to plant some surveillance equipment, keep an eye on the place that way."

"Yeah," said Clare. "But suppose the thieves nicked it?"

Ben laughed. He seemed like a nice guy. Clare wondered why it was that he and Jan didn't get on. Then she found herself thinking about Neil.

"It must get lonely in that warehouse, all on your own."

She was thinking aloud, but Ben replied.

"I can't see you worrying about Neil getting lonely," he muttered, out of the side of his mouth.

Clare flinched.

"He should be over that by now," she mumbled.

"Maybe," said Ben, in a tone which suggested that he'd already said too much, "but he isn't."

A call came in on the radio.

"Burglary on Nuthall Road. Suspects escaped in a dark blue Ford Escort. Heading towards city."

Ben spoke into the mike.

"5117 responding."

He turned to Clare.

"Dark blue Escort. Sound familiar?"

Then he put his foot down, and they were on their way.

Ben headed straight for the ringroad, swerving through changing traffic-lights, reaching the big intersection with Nuthall Road just as the dark blue car charged through, against the lights. Clare switched on the siren as Ben followed, almost skidding on the road surface, which was already beginning to ice up.

Clare had never been in a car chase before. This wasn't like the movies. Neither the car they were in nor the one that they were chasing had a great deal of power. And there was nothing else on the street: no need for acrobatic stunt steering between parked cars and busy traffic.

Nevertheless, it was exhilarating. The car strained as Ben kept it in low gear, only yards from the vehicle they were chasing. Clare knew from the radio that there were two more police cars about to intercept them. Maybe the thieves knew it, too. All but the least professional carried scanners these days.

Then, just as suddenly as it had begun, the chase ended. A second Panda rocketed out of Gregory Boulevard, blocking the Escort's path. It swerved, hit a traffic bollard, then span round, stranded in the centre of the street, its headlights smashed in. Ben pulled up yards away from it.

Clare prepared to get out of the car. None of the others did. Perhaps they thought that the car was about to escape again, but Clare could see that one of its tyres was torn to shreds. The black guy in the balaclava tumbled out of the car now, followed quickly by the white one. He and Clare exchanged glances.

"Hello again, Sean," she said. "Remember me?"

Neil shivered and poured himself some more coffee from the flask his mother had made him. He couldn't allow himself to drift into sleep any more, not now that he was on his own. He would be too vulnerable.

To fill in time, he tried to work out what he knew about the operation:

1. Garden Street was a temporary storage place and could not be traced back to the gang(s) using it. The place was for rent and the owners were cooperating

with the police surveillance operation.

2. The burglars who had been caught (by Ben and Jan Hunt, amongst others) didn't know the next link of the chain. They were paid by a middleman, who the police had yet to identify.

3. The captured burglars had been promised the recommendation of lighter sentences if they kept their silence. So far, this seemed to have held, as more goods had been deposited in Garden Street.

4. The police had no idea where the stuff was going on to. The quantities involved were too large for car boot sales or market stalls like the one where Clare's brother's computer had been recovered. It was possible that the middleman supplied specified goods from 'shopping lists' sent in by bent customers, but Neil didn't think so. There had to be a bigger market of some kind.

5. The way Neil saw it, there had to be another warehouse, or storage space, one that the actual thieves knew nothing about. If this was, as CID suspected, a vast fencing operation, there had to be a "Mr Big" behind it, someone who probably looked legitimate. Neil would love to help capture him – a collar like that would help him get a transfer to CID.

6. There was no number six. The captured thieves refused to name or identify the middleman who paid them, for fear (they said) of their lives. All they had been told was to take the stuff to the Garden

Street warehouse. But they weren't meant to go there straight from a job, just in case (as happened here) they were secretly followed. Now, all the police could do was to wait for a break.

Neil heard a noise, coming from outside, but didn't get excited. The night was full of noises. Then there was a scraping noise, the sound of a key turning. Neil switched on his radio.

It was dead.

Sean Dawes had been cautioned and waived his right to a lawyer. His partner, Solomon James, was remaining silent, but Dawes didn't know this. Sergeant Cope, conscious that neither Ben nor Clare were very experienced with interrogation, was sitting in. CID had been informed of the two men's capture, but had expressed no interest, unless Dawes seemed likely to implicate anyone involved in passing on stolen goods.

"Where did you sell the stuff on to, Sean?"

"A black man on the Green."

This was the standard answer.

"What was the man's name?"

"No comment."

This was the other standard answer. Clare and Ben glanced at each other. Ben nodded.

"You remember the robbery you did in Bobbers Mill, Sean, the one where you were interrupted?"

Sean looked at her. Earlier, he hadn't seemed to recognize her, although he had admitted burgling the Coppolas and several other places.

"I already held my hands up to that."

"You see…" Clare spoke softly, giving the impression of a meek, nervous, newly-qualified PC – which, to some extent, she was.

"It was you, wannit? You lived there?"

"That's right. The thing is, Sean, we know that you didn't sell the proceeds of that burglary in Hyson Green, because some of it turned up in Sneinton Market. The computer."

"So?"

"We know who you sold it to, Sean. His name's Paul Smetton."

"Never heard of him."

"The question is … what did you do with the rest of it?"

Sean was silent. Ben repeated the question. Maybe, Clare thought, he isn't as small time as he appears. Maybe he's the lead that we've all been looking for. She looked at Sergeant Cope. It was time, she thought, to change the subject. She wanted to talk about Hannah Brown.

"It'll be a lot easier on you, Sean, if you tell us what you did with the stuff," Sergeant Cope said, in a fatherly tone.

Sean sneered.

"I want a solicitor," he said.

The interview ended at 2.10 a.m.

Neil had checked the radio when he came on duty.
Hell, he had double-checked it. But now he
couldn't get it to work. He banged it against the
floor and got a brief burst of noisy static. Quickly,
hoping that the men coming in hadn't heard, he
switched it to "talk". The light didn't even come on.

Neil cursed silently as he watched the shadowy
men begin to lift videos and TVs from the shelves.
It looked like they were taking everything. He
checked his watch. Presuming that nothing was
going down, the patrol car with Ben Shipman and
whoever was partnering him would come round
about once an hour. Sometimes, not always, it
would come down this street. They had been
warned not to make their interest in the warehouse
look too conspicuous.

Neil warmed his radio against his chest, trying to
heat the batteries back into life. It didn't work. The
men were moving quickly, without talking. Neil
guessed that they knew the warehouse was no
longer a safe place to store stolen goods. The men
who Ben and Jan captured here might not have
talked, but they wouldn't have gone for their money,
either. The middleman would have got suspicious.
Tonight could be the last chance to find out where
the stolen goods were going. And he was having to
sit here, watching them get away with it.

They were nearly done. Neil made up his mind. As quietly as he could, he left by the back entrance. The movers were making too much noise for them to hear him. There was a phone box on Ilkeston Road, but Neil had to find something out first. He hurried round on to Garden Street, where the van was parked. The back doors were open. It looked nearly full.

Neil memorized the registration number, then ducked into a doorway as the men came out again, bearing yet another load. He calculated: three minutes to run to the phone box. Then a minimum of two minutes after he rang in before the message went out on the radio. But sometimes it took over a minute before the three nines call was put through.

He was going to lose them. Damn it. He was going to lose them.

Neil watched as the men went back in for what must be the last time. It was time to chance it. He ran, grateful that he was wearing trainers, not heavy PC Plod shoes. He could see torch lights moving about inside the warehouse as he passed.

Neil got into the back of the van. It was nearly full, but hadn't been loaded with much care. The men were in a rush. There were several blankets and sheets of plastic around, presumably to cover the stuff and prevent it from getting scratched. Neil picked one of the blankets up.

Behind him, Neil could hear the men returning.

He pushed his way as far back as he could, squeezed into a corner, and pulled the blanket around him. His heart stopped beating for several seconds as they shoved the last few things into the back. Neil overheard their conversation.

"Lock it?"

"Nah. Bring the padlock with us. We don't want anyone screwing up, leaving more stuff there."

The doors slammed shut. Then Neil heard the men getting into the front of the van. A moment later, the engine started up. They were on their way.

Neil knew that, if the men decided to unload the van at the other end, he was in real trouble. But if they didn't, he was in clover.

It was a very big if.

19

The duty solicitor didn't show up until half past three, and then took fifteen minutes consulting her client. Ben and Clare agreed that there was no chance she would allow Dawes to talk about his fence. Therefore, at 3.47, they went in on a different tack.

"Tell me about Hannah Brown," Clare said, the moment the interview began. Dawes looked confused.

"You what?"

"Hannah Brown, the girl I saw you with last Saturday night."

"Are you off your head?"

"Perhaps you didn't notice my face, Sean. Or perhaps you'd had a lot to drink. But presumably you remember tripping me up, then punching my colleague, who was also a police officer, before running away when she set off a personal safety alarm."

A look of understanding spread across Sean's face.

"Ah," said Sean. "You mean Mandy."

Clare remembered the name that Hannah had been using the first night she saw her. She hadn't been sure, until now, that it was the same girl. The solicitor spoke up.

"Is my client being charged with an offence here?"

"Not at this point," the sergeant said.

"I didn't know you were police," Sean protested. "Not then. Later on, Mandy, she told me she were a runaway, she were only fifteen. But I didn't know that, then. And I didn't do nothing with her, either."

"Tell me about her," Clare said, gently. "Where did you meet?"

Sean began to tell them.

The journey didn't take long. Four, five minutes, maybe, driven at a steady speed. They juddered to a halt, and Neil found himself praying, even though he didn't believe in God, praying that they wouldn't unload the van straight away.

He could hear a door being opened, one of those metal slide-over ones. The van moved forward a little. Then it stopped. Neil shivered.

He heard the men getting out of the front of the van. He heard their conversation, but couldn't quite make out the words. Then he heard the back door of the van rattle.

Please God, I'll do anything.

The door opened.

Neil cowered in the corner, trying to work out what to do. He should have been ready. He should have been ready to jump out the minute the door was opened, surprising the men, then either arresting them, or running away. But he wasn't ready. He was still hidden in a corner, hoping to escape discovery.

"Is it all right?" he heard one of the men say.

"It'll do."

The doors slammed shut and Neil breathed again. They were only checking the load. He heard the sliding door come down and assumed that they had gone. Nevertheless, he waited five more minutes, taking in the silence, thinking, preparing to make his move.

Finally, he crept between the piled up Panasonics and Sonys, edging his way to the door, exhilaration building up. He began to imagine the booty he would find when he got out of the van.

Neil wasn't an overly ambitious or big-headed copper, but he found himself imagining the commendation for bravery which would be awarded when he, personally, uncovered the biggest fencing ring in the history of Notts...

Then he thought about Clare Coppola and how she would feel when she realized what kind of man she'd given the boot to.

Then he reached forward to open the van doors.

They were locked.

"She weren't that interested in me," Sean moaned. "After I let on what I did, she were on about burgling all the time. Wanted to know all about the life."

"And how much did you tell her?" Clare asked.

The solicitor leant over and spoke into Sean's ear. He nodded.

"I told her a lot. Some of it weren't true. It were – what do'y'call it? – exaggerated. I thought it was turning her on, like, but it didn't get me anywhere. She spent half the night going on like she wanted us to be Bonnie and Clyde, then, when I tried to get her clothes off, she gives me this sob story. She were only fifteen. She were homeless. She were tired. She'd got a cold."

"What happened then?"

"She went to sleep. So did I. Next day, same thing. She wanted to know everything I did. She wanted to meet people. I took her to the pub, brought her home, ended up sleeping on the floor in my own flat. When I woke up, she were gone. End of story."

Clare looked at Ben. Earlier, he had shown no interest in Hannah Brown's disappearance, but now his eyes were animated.

"What sort of questions was she asking, Sean? Can you remember?"

"Same sort you lot ask me. Wanted to know how we chose houses, where we took the stuff after. She kept asking names, too, like she was going to write a book about it."

"Did you give her any?"

"A couple. I'd had a few drinks, hadn't I? But, you know, I don't know that much. I'm not really connected. Anyway, if I see that little bitch again, I'll kill her."

"Why?" Clare asked. "She did you no harm."

"Oh, yes, she did," Sean complained. "I only realized the day after."

"What?"

"The little tart nicked my camera."

Hannah checked her watch. It was twenty-nine hours since she'd last eaten. It was too cold to sleep. Her holdall had probably been found by now, and handed in or stolen. All she had were the clothes she was wearing, which were torn, and the contents of her handbag.

She had a black eye and her body was bruised in several places where Greg had hit her. She had learnt a lesson. You didn't pick up strange men in bars then go back to a deserted warehouse with them. She had learnt the lesson the hard way.

But she had also found out what she wanted to know.

There was a filthy tarpaulin which Hannah had carried with her when she fled from the warehouse twenty-four hours earlier. Greg looked for her for a while after she ran off, but quickly gave up. He was drunk and cold. He had taken the van out, locked up, then driven home to his wife while Hannah, only a few yards away, watched.

A day later – only a few minutes ago – the van had returned. Greg and another man were in it. The other man was the one who had given Greg the keys in the club the night before. They were in the warehouse for less than five minutes, then locked up. They left in a car which must have been parked earlier in the day, while Hannah slept her exhausted sleep. She didn't know what they were doing in the warehouse at that time of night, but she could guess.

While they did this, Hannah took several photographs. They probably wouldn't come out, but she was using a fast film – it was worth a try. Another three hours and it would be daylight. She put the camera back into her handbag. It was an expensive compact with a zoom. It was supposed to be good. She had seen it endorsed in magazine advertisements by a second-rate film director. She wondered who it had been stolen from, before she stole it from Sean.

Then she watched, and waited.

Hannah checked her watch again. It was twenty-nine and a quarter hours since she'd last eaten. Her stomach gurgled and her cough was getting worse. How much longer would it be? How many more hours could she last?

She pulled the tarpaulin more tightly around her and waited for dawn to come.

20

Neil must have slept. He had spent an age trying to force the van doors open and failed. Then he curled up in a corner with the filthy blankets wrapped around him and tried to get warm. He failed at that, too.

Yet, somehow, he had slept. Now his arms ached, his legs had gone to sleep, and his back felt like someone had been walking all over it. Something had woken him up. What? Were those voices he could hear, or just a heating system coming to life on a cold Monday morning?

Neil heard the van being unlocked and he was sure. They were voices.

The van doors opened.

The first voice was one from the night before.

"Can't be too careful, eh."

The second voice wasn't.

"You made a pig's ear of loading this van."

"I know, but nothing broke. We were in a hurry."

"It looks like it."

Neil felt he recognized the second voice, which now spoke again.

"You're sure you weren't followed?"

Where had he heard it?

"Positive."

"And you left nothing behind?"

It was somewhere recent, on a case.

"Nowt. Have you got somewhere new lined up?"

"Not yet. We've enough stock to keep us going for three or four weeks. Let the tea-leaves keep their pickings at home for a while, get a little paranoid. Then we'll buy the lot up cheap in time for the Christmas rush."

The first man laughed. There was a pause.

"Want to help me unload this lot?" the first man said. The other laughed.

"You must be joking? And get this suit dirty? Anyway, I haven't had breakfast yet. You do it. Take your time. The lorry won't be along to collect until ten. Here."

Neil couldn't hear, but guessed that money was changing hands.

"Thanks."

Neil crossed the fingers of both hands. If the boss

was leaving, then it would be just him and the other bloke. And the warehouse door was open – must be, because there was daylight streaming in. If the first guy went off to make a cup of tea or something, maybe Neil could get away without a fight.

It had gone quiet. Probably, the first man was seeing the second man off. Slowly, Neil stood. He had to get some circulation back into his veins before he made his escape.

Still quiet. Neil stretched his legs, began inching his way towards the door. All he could see beyond was a grey darkness and dingy daylight, revealing what might be a road, or a car park.

His back ached. Everything ached. He rubbed his hands together, tried to feel each of the toes in each of his feet, then moved a little closer to the doors. Soon he was hiding behind the left door, shielded by it, listening, getting ready to make his run.

Suddenly, there were voices. The second man, the boss, hadn't gone yet.

"What's all that mess in there?"

"That'll be Greg. I gave him the keys, Saturday night. He needed somewhere to take a bit on the side."

"*A bit on the side?* What do you think this is, a knocking shop?"

"Sorry. It won't happen again."

"Bloody right it won't. I don't want some tart knowing what's kept in this place."

"You know Greg. He wouldn't have given any-thing away."

"He'd better not have. Or it won't just be his wife who wants to chop…"

Go, Neil pleaded silently. *Go on, get out of the way. Give me time to leave.* Still he couldn't put a face to the second voice, the bloke who seemed to be in charge. It was bugging him. All he had to do was lean forward a little bit, take one quick peek, and he would know. It was dangerous, but it was hard to resist. *Go,* he insisted silently. *Walk past where I can see you!*

"Any word about…?"

No reply. The boss was either shaking his head or ignoring the question. Neil couldn't resist any longer. He leant forward to sneak a look, caught the guy in profile. *Of course,* Neil told himself. He should have remembered. His mind raced into overdrive, trying to make connections. Something fell out of his jacket.

"What was that?"

Neil groaned. His radio had fallen from his jacket to the floor of the van, and bounced outside it. When he stood up, he had been too stiff to secure it properly. Then he had forgotten about it.

The radio crackled and Neil realized that the mistake might be about to cost him his life. There was a rush of static, followed by the voice of the Control Room Operator. She was reading out Neil's badge number.

"This officer is missing and may have been gone for some time. Please call in any relevant information immediately."

The door swung open. Neil found himself looking at a familiar face, a middle-aged man with evil in his eyes.

"Well, well, well," the man said, "what have we here?"

The man shook his head slowly. Neil thought about running, calling for help, but it didn't seem like a good idea. He stood no chance.

"You know me, don't you?" the middle-aged man said. "You know who I am and what I do?"

"Yes," Neil replied.

"In that case," the man said, without a flicker of emotion, "you're dead."

21

The shift was over, but Clare stayed on, typing up her notes of the Sean Dawes interview. A search warrant had been applied for, allowing them to go through his flat.

So far, they had learned nothing conclusive about the missing girl. Hannah Brown was fascinated with crime, and had stolen a compact Olympus camera which had itself been stolen from a house in the Park. Sean had no idea where she was, and only limited ideas about where she had been staying. She had said nothing to him about her life being in danger.

Across the parade room, Tim Cooper was fiddling with the portable TV set, trying to get the morning news, finding only the Big Breakfast. Ben

Shipman was still here too. He was talking to Sergeant Crier, who headed the morning shift. Crier was saying:

"There's probably a simple explanation. He got fed up, went home, then the gang came and emptied the place. Have you rung his home?"

"No. We don't want to upset his mum. I know Neil, he wouldn't have deserted his post."

At the mention of Neil's name, Clare's ears pricked up. Inspector Grace came in, wearing a posh mac. He was also meant to be off duty.

"Sod CID," Grace said. "Foster didn't make contact once after two, no routine call-ins. They contacted him once at five, no response. They said they assumed his battery was dead. A lot of the radios have been playing up lately. In that case, I told them, why didn't you go by, get him a new one? There wasn't time, they said. The shift was nearly over."

Now Clare grasped the situation and found herself trembling. She turned to Grace, who gave her what, for him, was a compassionate look.

"What do you think, boss?" Her voice was unnaturally quiet.

"I think they've got him," Grace replied, bitterly. "And I don't know what we can do about it."

He began thinking aloud.

"That bloke in custody. Do you think if we had another go…?"

Clare shook her head.

"He doesn't know any more than we've found out already."

Grace nodded.

"CID are rounding up the two blokes who were caught in the warehouse in the first place, but they're not optimistic."

"Clare?"

It was Ben.

"Phone."

It couldn't be her parents. She'd rung Dad, the early riser, told him she'd be late.

"I'm not on duty. Get someone else."

A moment later, Ben came back.

"He says his name's Mike. Says it's urgent."

Reluctantly, Clare picked up the phone. The last person she wanted to talk to now was Mike Butler.

"Mike, I'm sorry, we're in the middle of a bit of a crisis here."

"I understand, Clare. Listen, I've got a bit of a crisis here, too. I'm at the flat. Hannah Brown's with me. She rang me half an hour ago and I've just picked her up. She wants to talk."

"That's great," Clare said, "but I'm afraid she'll have to wait. Look, Mike, Hannah's led us a merry old dance and I'd like to tell her what I think of her. But I'm off duty. I'm only here because one of my colleagues is missing. Someone will come for Hannah, but it might be a while. We're very busy."

"You really ought to get someone here soon," Mike said. "She's got an interesting story to tell, from the little I've heard. She can shed light on a lot of crime in the city…"

"Great," Clare said. "Keep her there. Now I've got to go."

She hung up on him.

Ted Brown and the other man bundled Neil into a small room with a table, a chair and a filthy mattress. A two-bar electric fire took the chill off the air. Brown used Neil's own handcuffs to lock him to the chair. Then they left him there.

"How did you get here?" Hannah Brown's father asked, when they returned.

Neil didn't reply.

"Does anyone know you're here?" Brown asked.

Neil kept silent. It could be that his best hope of survival was if they thought the cavalry were coming. He stared at the two men: Brown, wearing an expensive suit which didn't disguise that he was a short, overweight man, thinning hair combed back, eyes bulging out of his head like a demented fighting dog. The other was younger, taller, in jeans, with a leather bomber jacket, gold chain beneath a prominent Adam's apple, heavy gold rings on his fingers. He looked dangerous.

"Let's start again, shall we?" Brown said, softly.

Then he punched Neil in the face, hard. Neil

could feel his nose breaking.

"How did you get here?" he asked, voice turning sarcastic. "Were you waiting in the warehouse, or did you just happen to be passing?"

Neil said nothing. He felt the blood dripping on to his uniform. He knew that, in a moment, Brown would hit him again.

This time, it was in the mouth. At least it's not the other guy, Neil thought. With those rings, he'd split my lip.

"Who else knows you're here?" Brown asked.

"Why don't we take it in turns?" Neil replied, his voice sounding different to him as he spoke, distorted. "You could tell me why your stepdaughter ran away. Did she find out what you were up to, threaten to expose you?"

Brown hit him again. Neil spat out a tooth.

"You want to be careful," he said to Brown. "You're getting blood on your suit."

Brown kicked him and took a step backwards. Then the other man spoke.

"If anyone knew where he was, they'd be here already, wouldn't they?"

Brown said nothing, but watched Neil for his reaction. Then he looked at the sleeve of his jacket. Neil wondered if he was thinking about the dry-cleaning bill, decided not to crack a joke about it.

"I'll call Greg," he told the other man, not

bothering to lower his voice or get out of earshot. "Tell him to come over with his shooter. You finish unloading the van, then we can use it to shift the body. I want him out of here before the lorry arrives. All right?"

He made arranging for Neil's death sound like ordering a pizza.

"Right," his sidekick replied.

"And make sure you gag him."

Brown stared at Neil's bleeding face and Neil was sure he was going to hit him again. But Brown didn't. As he left the room, however, he unplugged the electric fire. *Now I've got a choice,* Neil thought. *I can wait to get shot or I can freeze to death.*

"There's really nothing for you to do here," Inspector Grace told Clare and Ben. "You might as well go home, get some sleep."

"I couldn't sleep," Clare said.

"Me neither," Ben chipped in.

"Then make yourselves useful. Go and pick up the Brown girl before she skips off again. We've wasted too much time on her not to get a result."

"I don't know," Clare said. "What if...?"

"If anything comes in about Neil, I'll radio you. Now, if you want me to authorize your overtime, I want you to pick up Hannah Brown, take her home. All right?"

"We're on our way," Ben assured him.

It was odd, Clare thought as Ben drove them to the Lace Market: a fortnight ago, she'd been desperate to find Hannah Brown. Now, it was just another case, something to take her mind off what was happening to Neil. When she thought about her ex-boyfriend, she was swept up in a jumble of emotions. People talked about the dangers of police work, and she accepted that they were part of the job – in the abstract – but when someone you knew … someone you *loved* was in mortal danger, everything became frighteningly real.

Ben parked on a single yellow line.

"Which one is it?"

"Up there."

Mike opened the door.

"She's in here."

He showed Ben and Clare into the living-room. Clare found herself facing a tired-looking girl with brown, unkempt hair and a pale, bruised face. She wore a black tracksuit which was far too large for her and must belong to Mike. Her face, without make-up, still had some baby fat to it. She looked her age, not quite sixteen. She was coughing. And she was scared.

"Hannah's suffering from pneumonia," Mike said. "And she's taken a beating. Really, she ought to be in bed."

"I know you," Hannah said, quietly, as she looked at Clare.

"We ran into each other a couple of times," Clare said, tactfully.

"No, I don't mean that. I only realized who you were when I found out your name. Then I remembered where I'd seen you."

"And where was that?"

"Last year. At Angelo's funeral."

"Aah. I didn't know that you and he were friends," she said.

"We weren't. I didn't like him much. He was one of those show-off, selfish kids, always wanted attention in class, always going on about computers or football, a real pain in the neck."

Clare smiled.

"Yes, he was." Then added: "So why did you go to the funeral?"

Hannah shrugged.

"I guess I felt guilty, for not liking him. And upset, about the way he died. You never know, he might have turned out all right, in the end."

"You're right," Clare said. "You never know."

Then she looked more closely at Hannah.

"How could you let yourself get into a state like this? I don't know why you left home, but it can't have been worth what you've been through."

"Oh, it was," Hannah insisted. "It was."

But Clare wasn't having any of it.

"What you probably don't realize," she told Hannah, "is that you've been lucky. The city's full of men who prey on people like you. Look at the risks you've taken – picking up sordid blokes in nightclubs – you were fortunate that Sean Dawes didn't turn out to be more violent, as well as being a thief. Even Mike here … you should never have come back to this place with him on his own. Didn't your mother teach you anything?"

Hannah shrugged.

"Not things I really needed to know," she told Clare. "Is the lecture over? Because there are a few things I'd like you to know."

Clare gave an exasperated sigh. Ben spoke.

"What do you want to tell us?"

"I want to tell you why I left home," Hannah said.

22

The story that Hannah told over the next few minutes came out in a rush. Some of it, Clare knew already. But much of it was a bolt from the blue. She, Ben and Mike listened, without interrupting until Hannah got near to the end.

Hannah loved her father and he adored her. He was away a lot, but that only made the times when he was at home more special. Hannah built up this image of him as a righteous crusader for justice and, though she was dimly aware that there was friction within her parents' marriage, she felt happy and secure.

Then he died. Only somebody who's been through it can understand the pain, anger and despair which a senseless, accidental death brings.

Clare understood. For a while, Hannah told herself (for no reason) that he had been murdered. It was a form of denial. Later, she turned against her father's memory, convinced that he had recklessly caused his own death. Eventually, she became numb.

Her mother married Ted Brown the summer before Hannah started secondary school, a little over a year after Mike Knight's death. Ted and Mike had been in the Masons together. He was divorced. Hannah took his name. Like many girls of that age, she was acutely conscious of not wanting to seem "different" – having the same name as the people you lived with was one way of seeming normal. But she never loved her new stepfather, and grew apart from her mother.

The Knight family were comfortable, but the Brown family were well off. Hannah was never one of those girls who wanted a pony, or any pet, but, if she asked, she was given. It got so she wouldn't mention liking things or she might find the next day that she owned them. This made her more uncomfortable.

As Hannah grew older, and intelligent enough to rationalize her feelings, she decided that they were to do with her father's death. She had been brought up in one life and abruptly moved to another. When Mum married Ted Brown, they lost touch with friends made through the police. They moved house and Hannah lost friends too. She made new friends and pretended that everything was all right. In a way, she believed the pretence. Scratch the surface of anybody's family and you found problems. Slowly, she realized that there was more to it than that.

Ted Brown rarely talked about business at home. He was away a lot, often abroad on "buying" trips. He never took Hannah to his stores. Now and then, though, there were late-night outings, cryptic phone calls. By the time she was fourteen, Hannah had become suspicious. She began watching, and waiting.

Hannah made her move while Ted Brown was away on a prolonged trip to the new European countries which used to be in the Eastern bloc. She persuaded Mum to get her a job at the Bonanza superstore. It was an ordinary, boring job. Hannah's suspicions faltered. Probably, she thought, countless teenagers suspected their parents of being criminals. She was suffering from normal teenage paranoia.

But then she started noticing things: deliveries, unusually, on a Sunday, men who came in more than once and seemed to hang around, not buying anything. The stolen credit card was the clincher. From the guy's manner, Hannah suspected that it was stolen. She made an excuse to go over to the office, have it checked out. But no one seemed to want to do anything about it. Finally, a little agitated, the manager rang it through and – no, it was fine. Only, when Hannah went back to the till, the guy who'd presented it had run off. The guy had been Sean Dawes.

Later, it turned out that the credit card had been stolen but not yet reported. Hannah was congratulated, but not in a convincing way. The next week, her stepfather returned and insisted that she packed the job in. He said that her doing it "embarrassed" him and upped her allowance instead. But Hannah began going back there, watching, trying to work out what was going on.

Later, when she found Sean Dawes, she realized that he had nothing to do with her stepfather. If he had, he would have known which till to go to with the stolen credit card. When the police raided Sean Dawes' flat, they would find that he still had Maria Coppola's jewellery stashed away beneath the floorboards, because he didn't know a fence who he could sell it to.

Gradually, Hannah worked it out. Her father's two shops were mainly outlets for stolen property. He did enough legitimate business to stop anyone being suspicious, and his status as the second husband of a police widow didn't hurt either. But the majority of his profits came from crime and the majority of people in senior positions in his shops knew exactly what was going on.

Hannah kept diaries and she took photographs. But she couldn't decide what to do about it all. There was nobody she felt she could confide in. Her mother either knew, or had deliberately decided not to know. They had lost touch with her real father's side of the family. Anyway, she was dependent on Ted Brown for her home, for the good standard of living they had. She had everything to lose.

Hannah did try to bring up the subject with her mum, but never got anywhere. Time and again, she tried to explain to her friends, but couldn't get the words out. Then her mind was made up for her.

It was a Sunday evening, sixteen days earlier. Hannah had been out, not spying on the Bonanza Electrical superstore that day, but visiting her friend, Amanda Perry. She'd arranged to stay the night and travel to school with Amanda the next day, but then Amanda's boyfriend showed up, and Hannah judged it tactful to return home instead.

She let herself in and saw Mum in an armchair, sleeping off the wine she'd drunk with Sunday dinner. So Hannah went upstairs. She assumed that Ted Brown was out. When she saw the light on in her room, she thought she must have left it on herself. Then she opened the door to find Ted going through her things.

For a moment, he didn't see her, so absorbed was he in what he was reading. Her diaries and note-books were open around him – secret details of her innermost thoughts and feelings, an account of her relationship with her first boyfriend and – scattered amongst them – her suspicions about her stepfather's business. Photographs taken secretly behind the superstore showed goods being delivered by vans and lorries which bore no company name.

Suddenly, Ted Brown looked up and saw her. His face was red with anger. The veins in his neck twitched. Hannah was sure that he was going to hurt her. She didn't accuse him. She didn't need to. The accusation was contained in the diaries and photographs which were spread in front of him. He asked how many people she had told about this. She told him, truthfully, no one. Then she regretted the answer, wished that she'd lied, wished that she had told somebody, so that somebody could get her stepfather if he got her.

Ted Brown took the diaries, the photographs, even Hannah's camera, and told her that he was going to destroy them. Then he told Hannah that she was a crazy, paranoid, malevolent adolescent, and she needed treatment. He told Hannah that she had seen nothing which amounted to any evidence of wrongdoing. All she had was evidence of her fertile, freaked-out imagination.

Hannah asked him why, in that case, he was taking away all her stuff to destroy it.

Ted Brown pulled her very close to him, holding her closer than he had ever held her with affection.

He put his fingers around her throat. Then he told Hannah that if she ever told anyone – *anyone*, even her mother – her suspicions about him, then he would kill her.

Hannah believed him.

Ted Brown went out, taking her things with him. Half an hour later he returned, threw the bag into her room, and told Hannah that the contents were floating in the Trent. If she wanted them back, she'd have to jump in after them. Then he repeated his threat to kill her if she repeated the allegations she'd made about him in her diary.

Hannah decided to leave that night.

She had money in her bank account, but she didn't have a plan. She didn't even have a camera any more. Her only course of action was to betray her stepfather, but she had no evidence. Ted Brown was a clever man, with plenty of contacts. It would be easy for him to convince people that she was off her rocker. He had the influence – she feared – to have her institutionalized. She would find it very hard to convince anyone of the truth behind her departure.

She left no note. She didn't want Ted Brown to be aware that she was going to attempt to expose him. At first, in fact, she was in two minds over what to do. She thought about going to another city, starting another life. But walking away from the situation went against her nature. A plan began to hatch in her mind.

Hannah packed warm clothes, but also clothes that she could wear in the evening, in the town's clubs and pubs. With make-up and the right dress, Hannah could look five years older than she really was. She had seen some of the people involved in her stepfather's business. If she could get close to one or two of them, she might be able to get the evidence she needed.

It wasn't easy, but, once she'd left, she couldn't go back. Living on the street was harder than she'd ever imagined. Without help from her friends, she wouldn't have got by those first few days. There was no hardened community of homeless people, like you read about in books and newspapers, ready to teach her the law of the street. She got plenty of offers, but all from men, only interested in one thing. The exception was Mike Butler, who looked after her, and tried to give her advice.

Eventually, through luck as much as anything else, she found Greg, who she had seen before, delivering goods to Ted Brown's store. Through him, she found the warehouse where stolen goods were stored. It was near her father's first store, the MegaMart, on Palm Street.

Last night, Hannah had seen, and photographed, Greg and another man (who had been with him in the Skyy club on Sunday) drive a van into the warehouse and leave. That morning, she had seen the other man and her stepfather arriving separately, going into the warehouse, opening the van door.

"Something funny happened then," she told the police officers.

"What?" asked Clare.

By now she was on the edge of her seat, mind whirring with possibilities.

"I think that there was someone in the back of the van, someone who wasn't meant to be there. He dropped something and my dad and this other bloke suddenly went all heavy. I only caught a glimpse of the guy, as they were moving him into the back room, but he looked familiar."

"Could he have been a police officer?" Clare asked.

"I didn't really see his clothes. They were very dusty. He was a bit taller than my stepfather, thin, with short fairish hair. Quite good looking."

"Neil," Clare said. "That's where they're holding Neil."

Ben stood up.

"This warehouse," he said to Hannah. "Tell us exactly where it is."

"I'm coming with you," Hannah said.

Mike interrupted.

"I don't advise…"

The others ignored him. Clare was already speaking into her radio.

"Inspector? I think we know where Neil's being held."

She gave him the details, then they hurried to the car.

"What do you think they're going to do?" Clare asked, as their car hurtled out of the city, siren blaring.

Hannah hesitated.

"I think they were probably going to question him, then, when they were through, kill him."

"*Kill?*" Ben asked. "Do you think that your stepfather's capable of that?"

Hannah replied in a deadpan voice.

"Why do you think I left home?" she asked.

23

The room was bitterly cold. Neil's feet were numb. His face ached and his mouth felt like an open sore. He had only himself to blame, that was what hurt the most. If he'd gone for the phone instead of sneaking into the van. If he'd stayed hidden instead of trying to sneak a look at Ted Brown. If.

Don't risk your life for the sake of property. It was a rule they drummed into you during training. It was a rule that he'd ignored.

Neil had a ticket to see Notts County tonight, before he came on shift. They were playing Leicester City. A local derby. It ought to be a good match, but Neil wouldn't see it, would never even know the result. Pretty soon now, Neil would be dead, and there was nothing he could do about it. He was handcuffed and his legs were tied to the chair. He had no means of fighting back. He couldn't even talk his way out because they had him gagged, too.

Ted Brown was long gone. Now Neil could hear the van being unloaded on the other side of the door. Soon, his body would be in the back of that van, ready to be dumped in the Trent, or a wood, some place where it would take a while before it was found.

The noises through the door stopped. Neil thought he could hear muted conversation, tried to ignore it. He thought about his mother. He thought about Clare Coppola. He thought about his father, dead these two years. He tried not to think about himself.

The door opened.

There were two cars outside the warehouse already when they arrived. Another car was in the car park, right next to the closed metal door.

"Is that your stepfather's?" Clare asked Hannah.

"No," she told her. "That's Greg's."

There were six of them in the car park, not counting Hannah: Paul Grace, Bill Cope, Ben, Clare and two CID men in plain clothes whose names Clare didn't know. Inspector Grace said that more cars were on their way.

"I don't think we should wait. Neil might be in danger."

They began to discuss what should be done, everyone nervously talking at once. Bill Cope thought that the men inside should be given five seconds warning, then they should kick the door in. Paul Grace agreed. Clare listened without contributing. She'd only been in the force a few months. It wasn't her place to suggest tactics.

Hannah was standing on the sidelines, shivering in the cold grey morning as Ben and the sergeant walked over, preparing to break their way into the warehouse. On the road below, traffic was starting to build up. The working week was beginning. Hannah grabbed Clare's arm.

"Are they planning to rush the place?"

Clare nodded.

"I don't think they should," Hannah told her.

"Why?"

"Something Greg said on Saturday. I think he's got a gun."

"Are you sure?"

"Yes," Hannah insisted. "Why else do you think my stepfather sent for him? He wasn't there earlier."

Clare ran over to the male officers, told them what Hannah had told her.

"We'll have to hold on, then," Paul Grace said.

He radioed Divisional HQ.

"They've already got armed officers on their way," he told the others.

"What if he shoots Neil while we're waiting?" Clare said.

"If we let him know we're here," the inspector countered, "Neil may not be the only one he shoots."

Inside the room, the two men were arguing. The new guy was waving a gun around. Neil didn't know what size, a .38 maybe. It was probably an automatic. Neil didn't know much about guns. He only knew that they killed people.

The new guy was heavily built. He had curly hair and a fake tan and might have been one of the ones from the night before. He was saying:

"You know I haven't got a silencer. What do you think I am? A gangster? You want to get out of the room before I fire this thing? Because otherwise your ears'll ring for a fortnight."

The other guy shook his head.

"All I'm saying is – what if someone hears? There are a lot of people working round here."

"Not yet, there aren't."

"They're starting to arrive."

"They'll think it's a car backfiring."

"I wouldn't bet on it."

The new guy stopped waving the gun around and put it down on a chair.

"Look, Chris, all I want is to get this over with. I bought this shooter for protection, not to turn into Ted's hit man."

"Then let's do it sensible. Put him in the van, drive him somewhere quiet, secluded, do the job there."

"This place is quiet," the new guy insisted. "Ted said to do it here."

The one called Chris shook his head, like it didn't make sense.

"Are you sure that's what he said?"

"Yeah. After he finished telling me off for bringing that tart here on Saturday night, he told me to whack the policeman."

Chris laughed.

"*Whack* him, just like in an American movie, huh? I didn't know Ted talked that way."

"Yeah, well what he actually said was: you still got that gun? Go on over there and give it some exercise."

"It doesn't sound like Ted cared where you did the *whacking*."

"Maybe. Maybe not."

"This is a policeman we're talking about here, Greg. We're talking life, thirty years minimum. I don't want to take unnecessary risks."

Now Neil had both of their names: Greg and Chris. Not that it was likely to do him any good. He watched Greg thinking about it.

"Maybe we should phone Ted," Greg said, eventually.

He took a portable phone out of his pocket, pulled up the aerial, and dialled. Neil could dimly hear the answering voice at the other end. He heard Greg say the word "when?" then "get him to call me," before he pushed the aerial back down again.

"Not home yet," Greg told Chris.

"Come on," Chris said. "Let's finish unloading the van. That way, whichever Ted decides, we'll be ready to go. OK?"

Everyone was on edge. To make things worse, it was starting to rain. Visibility was rubbish. Soon, the big boys would arrive and Ben would be reduced to the role of bystander. He watched Clare Coppola, pale faced, looking like she was holding back tears. Neil could, Ben realized, be dead already.

Where were the armed officers? Ben stood near the door. He could hear noises inside the warehouse, things being moved. He had an idea. Quickly, he trotted over to Hannah Brown.

"You say you've been inside the place?"

"Some of it. I think I know where they'll be keeping him."

"Here."

He handed her his notebook.

"Sketch me as much as you remember. It might help when…"

He looked up. Two vans came up the driveway. One was a police van. The other ... Inspector Grace swore.

"Who brought them?"

It was an Outside Broadcast Unit belonging to Central Television.

Jan Hunt finally got Henry back to sleep. It had been a long night and she was ready to drop off again herself. How, she wondered, would they have coped if she'd been at work all night? Mind you, Kevin was even more used to dealing with lack of sleep than she was. She didn't know which was the worst slave driver: the police force or the National Health Service.

She lay in bed, savouring the quiet darkness. Her son was a blessing and she loved him. She was glad that they'd chosen for her to have the baby, glad for all the new love it brought into their lives. She was a different person now that Henry was here, less selfish, less judgemental and, yes, too tired all the time to remember what her personality used to be like.

Perhaps she was trying to do too much. Perhaps she ought to reconsider her career, as Kevin kept trying to persuade her. She thought about it. But then the alarm went and Henry started crying again. Cursing, Jan went up to the room and gave him some breast. When she got down to the kitchen, Kevin was making toast. He had the breakfast news on the television, which always irritated her.

"Do we have to have that on?" she said, instead of her usual, "morning, love."

"Watch. You might find it interesting."

Jan glanced at the screen. The newsreader was saying:

"…a siege at a warehouse on the outskirts of Nottingham. We believe that a police officer is being held by armed men."

The picture cut to a shot of the warehouse. Jan recognized it, an industrial area on the edge of her beat. Then the camera moved in on the reporter and Jan thought she recognized some of the people clustered behind him, too. Surely that was Clare, and Bill Cope, and … that couldn't be. The girl writing in the notebook looked remarkably like the missing girl, Hannah Brown.

"Police aren't giving any details at the moment because they don't want to endanger the security of the operation, but I can confirm that armed police are positioning themselves around the building. We don't know for sure if the hostage is alive or dead."

Who was the hostage? The picture cut back to the newsreader. Clare and Bill weren't supposed to be on duty at the moment. If they were there, it meant that someone from their shift…

"What are you doing?" Kevin asked.

"I'm putting my coat on."

"Wha...?"

"I should have been there last night."

"Rubbish."

"Maybe. But I'm going to be there now."

"What about Henry?"

"Call work. Tell them you can't come in because he's got croup."

"I can't do that."

"Why not? I just did."

Jan picked up the car keys and left him to it. If Kevin got his act together, he could probably get Dawn to look after Henry for a while, but he could work that out for himself. She got in the car. It was Neil, she was sure of that. He had been on duty in that other warehouse last night, alone. He was stupid and reckless enough to have a go. She ought to know. She tutored him.

The one called Chris had left his cellular phone in the small room and now it began to beep. Ridiculous. Neil was sitting opposite a gun and a phone and he couldn't lay his hands on either of them. The noise from the other side of the door stopped. Greg came back into the room and picked up the phone.

"Yeah."

If he strained, Neil could just make out what Ted Brown was saying.

"Have you done it yet?"

"Nah. I wanted to, but Chris said not to do it

here, to take him somewhere quiet. That's why I rang. Shall I…"

He didn't finish the sentence because he was interrupted by Chris coming into the room. Neil couldn't hear the rest of what Ted Brown said. He could only hear Greg's side of the conversation.

"You what?"

"You can't be serious."

"You're kidding."

He switched the phone off and stared at Chris.

"Ted says the police are outside. It's on the telly and everything. They've got the place surrounded. He says we're on our own."

24

"Here." Hannah handed the sketch to Ben, who glanced at it and took it over to Paul Grace, who handed it to the sergeant in charge of the Armed Response Unit. It looked like this:

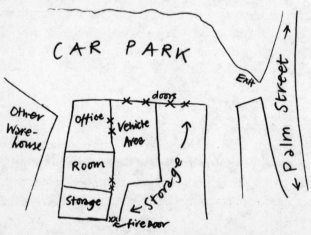

"You're sure that the corridor leading to the fire doors is clear?" the sergeant asked Hannah.

"It was on Saturday night. That's where I got out."

There were more hurried consultations. Paul Grace was trying to persuade the crew from Central to leave.

"You could be jeopardizing the whole operation!"

The reporter was having none of this.

"Oh, come on. You think they've got a TV on in there?"

"I can't be responsible if one of your people gets shot."

"No one's asking you to be."

This was Grace's first real crisis as an inspector, Ben realized. He didn't want to screw it up. The inspector turned to Ben.

"I'm going to use the loudhailer. If there's no response, the armed boys will go in. I want you to keep the unarmed people present shielded, behind the cars or behind that wall over there. Bill Cope will keep charge of the TV crew. Got it?"

"Got it."

Ben ushered Clare and Hannah into a secure position behind their patrol car. There was another police car outside the car park, there to steer away onlookers and prevent people from driving into the car park. Therefore, Ben was surprised when they let a green Citroen through. The car sped across the cracked concrete, parking directly behind where Ben and the others were crouching. Jan Hunt pulled down the window.

"You're just in time for the fireworks," Ben told her.

"Is it Neil in there?" Jan asked Clare.

"Yes. We don't know if he's still alive."

"What would be the point of killing him now? He's useful as a hostage."

"True. But they don't know that we're here yet, which makes him nothing but an awkward witness."

Jan looked at Hannah.

"What's she doing here?"

"Her father's behind all this. He's the biggest fence in Nottingham. That's why she ran away."

Ben watched Jan blink, taking it all in. Then he could see her thinking, calculating.

"Is Ted Brown in there?"

"We don't think so," Clare told her. "His car's not here."

"Is someone picking him up?"

This question was addressed to Ben.

"I don't think so," he replied.

"Then we ought to be. This is live on the news. He's probably noticed Hannah by now, knows that the game's up. He'll get away."

She was right, Ben realized. In the panic about Neil, no one had given any thought to Brown.

"Come on," Jan said to Ben. "Let's get over there."

"We can't just…"

Jan didn't let Ben finish.

"We haven't got time to wait for orders. Clare can explain to the boss where we've gone. Are you coming, or am I going on my own?"

Ben didn't pause to think any further.

"I'm coming."

She was a sergeant, after all, and she was in the right.

"I'm coming too," Hannah Brown said.

"No," Jan told her. "It might be dangerous."

"He's my stepfather," Hannah said. "You wouldn't know about him if it wasn't for me. I want to be there when you take him."

"You don't mean 'when', you mean 'if'," Jan said. "All right. I suppose it might be useful to have you with us. Come on. Get in, both of you."

Ben glanced back at the shiny new Panda he had driven here in, but said nothing. Jan was sitting there with the engine running and, anyway, an un-marked car might be a smart move. As they drove away, the three of them could hear Paul Grace, speaking through a megaphone.

Chris and Greg were still arguing when the noise started up outside.

"*Armed Police. You are surrounded. You must leave the building immediately, throwing out any weapons you possess beforehand. I repeat…*"

Neil recognized the voice. It was his new boss. The inspector's presence meant that they knew Neil was inside. He had no idea how they'd found him, but he was profoundly grateful. Greg swore. Chris came over to Neil and started to untie him.

"What do you think you're doing?" Greg asked.

"We're taking him with us. He's our ticket out of here."

Paul Grace's voice penetrated the cold, airless room.

"You have one minute. After that, we will not be responsible for any injury which befalls you."

"Come on," Chris told Greg. "Help me."

Neil's feet were free now. The gun was still on the table. He could make a run for it, if his legs weren't numb, and his hands still handcuffed together... The two men bundled him into the main part of the warehouse. The van door was open. Chris got in, started the engine, then pulled Neil into the front seat next to him. Greg jumped in after them. He had a remote control in one hand and the gun in the other. He pointed the remote at the door. It began to open.

Suddenly, from behind them, there was a crashing noise, then the sound of running feet. The warehouse door was nearly up. Chris accelerated into it, the top of the van catching the edge of the door as it crashed through.

Neil caught a brief glimpse of it all: police cars,

men with rifles, TV cameras, even some spectators over by the wall. It was a circus.

Then the shooting started.

"That's his car," Hannah said as they pulled up outside the Brown house. "It looks like he's home."

"How do you want to play this?" Ben asked Jan.

"He'll probably make a run for it, so you'd better cover the back way. Are you sure he isn't armed, Hannah?"

"I doubt it. Why would he have sent for Greg if he had a gun of his own?"

"Good point," Jan said. "Now, I want you to stay in the car until we bring him out."

"No way," Hannah told her. "I started this and I'm going to finish it."

If Jan had been Clare Coppola, it might have been another thing. But she hadn't seen either of these officers before today. She wasn't going to let them steal her moment of revenge.

"It might be dangerous," Ben told her.

Hannah opened the car door.

"I've lived with him for six years. It's a bit late now to tell me that he's dangerous. I know. Anyway…"

She reached into the pocket of the tracksuit, fished out what she was after, and held it up.

"I've got a key."

Nothing had changed. Why should it have, in two

weeks? The place even smelt the same – a mix of cigarette smoke and air freshener. Funny how you never noticed the smell of a place when you lived there. Hannah couldn't afford to pause. The sergeant was right behind her. She knew where Mum would be, if she was home. So she walked across the hall, cool as anything, pushed the kitchen door open and announced:

"Hi, Mum, I'm home!"

Then watched her mother's jaw drop. Mum was in her dressing-gown, a whisky in front of her, even though it was only eight in the morning. The national news headlines were on the TV, but were being interrupted. A voice said,

"Now we return live for developments in the armed siege at…"

Mrs Brown put her arms round Hannah, hugging her.

"I've been so…"

Then she broke into tears.

"Mrs Brown," Jan said gently. "We need to see your husband."

"It's him, isn't it?" Linda Brown said bitterly. She pointed at the TV set.

"All this has got something to do with him and with you leaving, hasn't it?"

"Sort of," Hannah told her.

"Why didn't you come to me, Hannah? Why didn't you tell me?"

"I thought … I thought maybe you knew."

Mum shook her head.

"I may be stupid. I may be blind. But I'm not … I'm not … what he is."

For the first time, Hannah's mother seemed to see the bruises on her face.

"Did he hurt you? Was that him?"

"No. Not him."

Both of them were crying now. Hannah could hear a police siren. She thought at first it was coming from the TV, but then she saw a police car pulling up outside the house.

"I called the police," Mum explained to Jan and Ben, "when I worked out what was going on. He's upstairs, packing."

Jan motioned to Ben, who left the room. Then Hannah heard footsteps crashing down the stairs. Her stepfather appeared in the doorway, coat on, car keys in hand, his expensive leather travel bag slung over his shoulder. He glowered at Hannah, then at his wife. Jan stepped forward, put her hand on his arm.

"Edward Brown, I'm arresting you for the possession and handling of stolen property. You do not have…"

Hannah's stepfather pushed Jan away, ran to the front door, then saw the police car and changed his mind. Hannah smiled as he ran through the kitchen, opened the back door and charged out, straight into the arms of Ben Shipman. Then her attention was drawn by the announcer's excited babble and she stared at the TV screen.

Clare watched as the van hurtled into the car park. She could make out Neil, in the front seat, sand-wiched between the driver and the man with the gun. For a moment, she was sure that Neil was going to get shot, there were so many bullets flying around. Then she worried about herself. She was taking cover inside the car they had come in, but hadn't thought to duck. Still, she was out of range now. The van was at the car park entrance, smash-ing into the side of the police car blocking it off.

They were going to get away, Clare could see that now. Without really thinking, she turned the keys in the ignition, speaking as she did into her radio.

"I'm following the blue van, registration number Tango Juliet Victor, One zero zero Charlie. It's heading for Radford Road. I'm keeping my distance because one of the passengers is armed. No other cars are in a position to follow immediately. Request back up."

"Back up on its way," the radio responded. "Try not to lose them, but don't intercept either. Which way are they turning?"

"Right."

Clare swore. She sounded her siren but had to wait for a gap before she could force her way out on to the main road, making the rush hour traffic swerve around her. The van was careering down the middle of the road. Cars were sounding their horns. Already, the van had caused a Volkswagen to crash into the back of a BMW. Clare held her breath and took off after it, down the middle of the road, only just avoiding a pedestrian refuge.

Ignoring the red lights, the van charged across the ring road, over to Hucknall Road on the other side. Clare went after it, hearing another crash behind her. She could be up on charges for this, she realized: unqualified, unarmed, she was breaking every regulation in the book. She didn't care. Neil was trapped in the van ahead with an armed man. She had to do what she could. The van veered off to the right and she followed, keeping it in sight, but keeping her distance too.

"We've got two cars a minute behind you," the radio told her. "Don't try and intercept the van. Repeat. Don't intercept. We have armed officers only a minute behind you."

A lot of good they've been so far, Clare thought.

The van turned off the main road. Clare was still a hundred yards behind. If it made another turn, she'd lose them. She pressed the right indicator, took a chance on forcing the traffic in the opposite lane to brake, then pulled across into the road where the van had gone. It was stopped, a few yards in front of her. Why? Clare was about to speak into her radio when she worked out what they must be up to.

But she was too late. The first gunshot hit one of her tyres. The second smashed the window. As the van started off again, the Panda veered off the road, straight into a lamp-post. Clare blacked out.

"Where are they going?"

The five people in the Brown kitchen had just watched the blue van escaping from the car park, pursued by a police car.

"How should I know?" Ted Brown said.

"They work for you. Come on. Where are they going?"

On the TV screen, the reporter was saying that there appeared to be no fatalities, but the criminals had escaped with their hostage. Paul Grace ran over, past the camera, up to the damaged police car. He was checking that the officers in it were all right. They were. Then he ran to the car he'd arrived in and was about to get in when the reporter hurried over to him.

"Inspector Grace. How would you say that the operation this morning has gone?"

Grace said two words which years of graduate fast track training should have warned him never to say on live television. Then he got in and slammed the car door in the reporter's face. A moment later, Jan heard his voice on her radio.

"Where are you, Sergeant?"

"I'm at the Brown house, sir. Mr Brown is under arrest."

"Well done. Look, I have to tell you, Clare Coppola's in that car. I didn't even know that she could drive…"

"She passed her test a month ago."

"Any idea where they're going?"

"Wait a moment."

Jan turned to Brown.

"You're done for. You know that. The only tiny hope you've got of us giving you mitigating circumstances in court is if you tell me *now* anything you know about where that van is heading."

Brown's eyes narrowed. Then he spoke.

"Greg's got a lock up. He keeps a car there. Maybe…"

He gave them the address.

Neil struggled in his seat, trying to see what had happened to the car which Greg had shot at.

"Knew her, did you?" Greg sneered and hit Neil on the chest with the butt of his gun. He had used five shots, Neil counted. That meant there was only one left. Unless … some guns had more than six bullets. He didn't know how to tell the difference.

Her. He had said *her.* Suppose it was Clare. The bastard might have killed Clare. What was she involved for? She shouldn't even be on duty. Tears began to fall down Neil's face, dampening the knotted cloth which prevented him from speaking. Neil blinked them back. He had to stay in control of himself, whatever happened.

They were driving across a council estate. Neil guessed that they had come a circuitous route in order to confuse the police cars following. Neither of the men spoke. Neil squirmed in his seat. The van radiator was on full. His legs had come back to aching life. He felt around behind him with his hands, trying to get some leverage. Suddenly, the van swerved. They were driving across a muddy track, towards some ramshackle garages.

Chris cursed.

There were three police cars, lining the only exit. A dozen armed officers stood there, pointing rifles at them. Chris hit the brakes.

"It's over," he said to Greg.

Greg didn't seem to agree. He pushed the van door open again and began to lean out, pointing the gun. Next to him, Neil pushed down with his feet, levered himself up with his cuffed hands, then threw the weight of his body at Greg's back.

Greg tumbled out of the van into the muddy morning, his gun going off as he fell. Half a dozen shots greeted him.

The van came to a halt. Chris, face pale as death, held his hands above his head. Neil manoeuvred his way out of the van; hands behind his back, legs aching, he stumbled to the ground, avoiding the bloodstained corpse which lay by the passenger door.

Behind him, he saw another police car pull up. While the armed police arrested Chris, Neil watched as Inspector Grace leapt from the car, then helped Clare Coppola to get out of the back seat. Clare saw Neil. Their eyes met with naked relief.

Smiling, and crying at the same time, they limped towards each other.

EPILOGUE

It was six in the morning, the end of November. Clare was the only one up. Even her father didn't rise this early when it stayed dark for so long. She stood in her brother's bedroom, looking around. Every object held a thousand memories: each book, the football posters and Subbuteo teams, the Monopoly game that he'd beaten her at so many times she'd refused to ever play him again. Over the last year and a bit, she had been in this room many times and had rarely left it without breaking down in one way or another.

Not today. She was saying goodbye. Mum was going to clean it out, she'd said the night before. Clare should take anything she wanted before she went back to Ryton. Clare looked around for a last time, then she reached over to the box marked "Sheffield United", the team which, for some unearthly reason, Angelo supported. She took out one of the Subbuteo players and put it into her coat pocket. Then she picked up her bag and went downstairs.

The night before, Mike Butler had rung her, asked her out for a farewell drink. Clare refused. She explained, as diplomatically as she could, that there was someone else. She'd thought that she was over him, but now she wasn't so sure. Mike said that he understood. They talked for a couple of minutes about Hannah, how she was trying to rebuild her life with her mother.

The heating hadn't come on yet and it was cold downstairs. Clare put her hands in her pockets, feeling the plastic figure which she'd just put there. She thought about Neil Foster, and whether they had a future together. She thought about Ruth Clarke, who she'd agreed to share a flat with when they returned to Nottingham, for good, in six weeks' time.

On the wall, in the living-room, was the commendation for bravery which Clare had received for her part in apprehending Ted Brown and his co-conspirators. Charges had been brought against twenty people and the case had been all over the papers for days. Clare still got pain from the cracked rib she'd suffered when she crashed into a lamp-post. But she'd recover. Her body was still young, and mended fast.

Clare heard a car pull up outside. She waved through the window, then hurried to the door, before the engine noise could disturb her parents, asleep upstairs. She opened and closed the front door quietly, then stepped into the street, which was white with freshly-fallen snow. Clare ignored the "For Sale" sign poking out from the house which had been her home for every one of her twenty years. The car door opened. Clare slung her bag on to the back seat, then sat down next to Ruth. They exchanged half-awake smiles before Ruth drove off, neither of them speaking.

Clare stared ahead at the falling snow flakes. In the distance, a police siren sounded. As they turned the corner on to Bobbers Mill Road, the siren grew louder. Then Ruth put some music on, drowning it out, and Clare wiped her eyes.

On the other side of the city, Hannah Brown slept soundly, in her own bed, at home.

Look out for the next exciting
instalment from

in
Black and Blue

Ben took the money from the machine, crossed the road, then began to jog up the hill, thinking about his girlfriend. He didn't see enough of her. In some ways, it was a miracle that they'd stayed together since finishing university. After all, she was in London and he was…

"There he is!"

Rapid footsteps behind him.

"Hold it right there, nigger!"

The last word made Ben tighten up inside. No one had used that word directly to him, not since he was at school. It made him want to stop, to hit out. Hard.

The sound of pounding feet grew louder. They were gaining on Ben, gaining all the time. But they wouldn't catch him. Ben knew this stretch of road better than he knew his home town. At the top of the hill he'd run into Mapperley Road, take a short cut down a dark alley. He'd be home before they sussed where he'd gone.

But Ben didn't get to the top of the hill. A white van careered across Mansfield Road, slamming on to the pavement, right in front of him. This wasn't casual, Ben realized. This was official. Which way to go? He glanced round to see how close they were.

"Gotcha!"

A white guy in an anorak rugby-tackled Ben to the ground. His mate came up from behind and landed a kick in Ben's stomach, knocking all the air out of him. Then the van door was opening and there was no point in fighting back because there were more of them in there too, only these ones were in uniform and they were dragging Ben into the van, heavy boots kicking him as they did. Then another face was in his, stripes on his shoulder. The stripes were shouting,

"We know you're not working alone. Where's your mate? Come on, you spook, tell us now. Where's your mate?"

Ben got back enough breath to mumble:

"I don't know what you're talking about."

A fist clobbered him in the side of the face, where a mark wouldn't show. Ben flinched. It was time to end this.

"What am I supposed to have done?" he asked,

through gritted teeth.

The sergeant sneered. There were beads of sweat around his ugly moustache.

"Don't take the—"

"Am I under arrest?" Ben interrupted him.

The plain clothes one who'd rugby-tackled him spoke now.

"Don't start telling us our job, scumbag. Show us your wallet."

Slowly, Ben reached into his jeans pocket.

"You lot ought to be under arrest," he said, handing the brown leather pouch to the CID man. "All of you."

"Let's take a look at your cash cards, shall we?" said the cocky plain clothes one who'd called him "nigger".

He opened the wallet and swore. Then his tone changed.

"Look, I'm sorry, mate. Nothing personal. You were in the right place and you fitted the description, all right?"

"What's going on?" the sergeant with the moustache wanted to know.

The guy in the anorak held out Ben's wallet so that the other three men could see the warrant card in it.

"That's right," Ben told them, not trying to hide the bitterness in his voice. "I'm a police officer."

Other books by David Belbin in

P●INT CRiME

AVENGING ANGEL

Traffic's murder tonight…

Clare and Neil of The Beat meet as they
investigate Clare's brother's death…

FINAL CUT

Lights, camera … murder…

SHOOT THE TEACHER

Even teachers don't deserve to die…

And look out for:

BREAK POINT

Game, set and … murder…